"You Never Thought You'd Meet Me Again, Did You, Eve?

"But you should have realized that there was bound to be a reckoning for what you did."

Before she could answer Luke, he pulled her against him and kissed her fiercely. The old madness began to flame through him, and suddenly he felt her press against him, not fighting him, but sliding her hands up until she could caress him.

Her lips were moving against his, seducing him with promises of infinite delight, delight such as he hadn't known since she'd left him. She was still the only woman who could make him feel as though nothing else mattered.

With a sudden jolt, he came back to himself and was assailed by fear. He'd been so sure of himself, yet already he was succumbing to her dangerous magic, ready to become her victim again.

Dear Reader:

I hope you've been enjoying 1989, our "Year of the Man" at Silhouette Desire. Every one of the twelve authors who are contributing a *Man of the Month* has created a very special someone for your reading pleasure. Each man is unique, and each author's style and characterization give you a different insight into her man's story.

From January to December, 1989 will be a twelve-month extravaganza spotlighting one book each month with special cover treatment as a tribute to the Silhouette Desire hero—our *Man of the Month*!

Created by your favorite authors, these men are utterly irresistible. Love, betrayal, greed and revenge are all part of Lucy Gordon's dramatic *Vengeance Is Mine*, featuring Luke Harmon as Mr. May, and I think you'll find Annette Broadrick's Quinn McNamara... *Irresistible*! Coming in June.

Don't let these men get away!

Yours,

Isabel Swift
Senior Editor & Editorial Coordinator

LUCY GORDON
Vengeance Is Mine

Silhouette Desire

Published by Silhouette Books New York

America's Publisher of Contemporary Romance

SILHOUETTE BOOKS
300 East 42nd St., New York, N.Y. 10017

ISBN: 0-373-05493-9

First Silhouette Books printing May 1989

LUCY GORDON

When asked about *Vengeance Is Mine*, Lucy said, "Perhaps we all delude ourselves about our feelings, but Luke Harmon does so more than most people. He's a man who has fascinated me for a long time, but I couldn't write about him until now because he needs to be explored from the inside. Throughout the book he makes a journey of self-knowledge, until he finally reaches the place where he's brave enough to confront his love for Eve."

In 1985 Lucy won the *Romantic Times* Reviewers Choice Award for Outstanding Series Romance Author. In 1987 she won a Golden Leaf Award from the New Jersey Chapter of the RWA for *Just Good Friends*, a Silhouette Desire, and in 1988 she was a finalist in the RWA Golden Medallion contest with her Silhouette Romance, *A Pearl Beyond Price*.

Prologue

The telephone on the desk in Luke Harmon's office rang. "It's her," his secretary said.

Luke didn't ask who. He knew it had to be Eve Drummond. "What did you tell her," he demanded sharply.

"That you'd speak to her. You said she was to be put through whenever she called, no matter what you were doing."

"Say I'll call back," he ordered abruptly, and slammed down the receiver.

He needed a few moments to calm himself. He'd been waiting for this call for ten years, and now that it had come his heart was beating and his throat was dry.

The walls of his luxurious office seemed to close in on him suffocatingly. He ruled a financial empire with an iron hand from this desk. People arrived eager to sell him their wares, and he received or dismissed them as the mood took him. Men sat in the chair opposite his, pleading with him not to destroy them, and he laid down his terms. Yet he was shaking because Eve Drummond had called.

Instinctively he raised his hand to the scar that just touched his left eye. It marred a face that should have been handsome. He was thickset, almost burly, with a muscular neck and large, powerful hands. But his dark eyes were unexpectedly fine and his mouth was mobile and sensitive. It was a face of contradictions, showing the strain of a nature that pulled one way and a cruel experience that pulled another.

He scarcely knew what he looked like. There were almost no mirrors in his home, and he contrived to shave without seeing the upper part of his face. In his whole life he could only remember once studying his own appearance, and that was when he'd asked himself anxiously if this was a man that Eve Drummond could love. Well, he'd had his answer. He touched the scar again.

At last he was sufficiently in command of himself to call her. "Thank you for calling back so soon, Mr. Harmon," she said. Her voice was husky, with a slight catch that he remembered. Luke grasped the receiver tightly, glad that she couldn't see how she affected him.

But none of the emotion he felt was revealed in his voice as he said coolly, "I've been expecting to hear from you, Miss Drummond. I believe you want to discuss the position of your late grandfather's company."

"Yes, as you can imagine, it was rather a shock to us to discover that you already held a controlling interest."

"By 'us' I take it you mean yourself and Parry Drummond, your second cousin."

She hesitated a fraction of a second, then, "You're very well informed. Mostly I just call Parry my cousin."

"But he is, in fact, your second cousin?"

She gave a rich chuckle. It was deeply feminine and alluring, and Luke's knuckles turned white on the receiver. "What a very precise man you are," she observed in an amused voice.

"I'm a businessman, Miss Drummond. I've learned to be precise about details. I'm sorry that Tyler never told you that he'd sold so many of his shares in Drummond, Inc."

"I knew he'd sold some, of course, but not a controlling interest."

"I see from the firm's records that some years ago Tyler signed over ten percent of the stock to Parry Drummond, and thirty percent to yourself. I assume you were expecting to inherit the remaining sixty percent between you."

"I, well, yes, but—"

"Instead of which I hold fifty-four percent, leaving you only a very small inheritance, I'm afraid."

"Mr. Harmon, it isn't the inheritance that's causing the problem. My lawyer tells me that you've refused to declare a dividend this year, effectively making our present stock holdings worthless."

"In my opinion a dividend wouldn't be justified."

"But surely you can see what a difficult position—oh, I can't talk on the telephone. Parry has been trying to contact you for weeks to discuss this, but you don't return his calls and you've refused to see him."

"So you thought you'd see if you could do better?"

"Well, at least I managed to get through to you, which is more than poor Parry has ever done." Her voice had a faint edge of amusement.

Luke managed to laugh, although his throat felt tight. "I'm sorry for my rudeness," he said. "Why don't you join me for a drink this evening?"

"I'd love to."

"Shall I send my car to collect you?"

"Thank you, but I prefer to arrange my own transportation."

He gave her the address of his apartment and added formally, "Eight o'clock then. I look forward to seeing you, Miss Drummond."

When Luke hung up, his hand was trembling with the violence of his emotion and the strain of hiding it.

Once, when he'd first known this woman, he'd been openhearted and eager, allowing every passing feeling to show on his face because he trusted her. But that was long ago. In the past ten years he'd become a master of concealment. No one knew of the craving for revenge that had been his driving force, and Eve Drummond mustn't be allowed to suspect that he hated her—not yet.

He returned home at seven-thirty that evening instead of working late into the night as he often did. His apartment was in the most expensive part of London. Its decor and furnishings had a clean, austere elegance that suited something bleak in his nature. The walls were white, adorned with modern paintings in steel frames. Luke, who knew little about art, and cared less, had inherited them from the previous owner and never gave them a thought.

He showered and then poured a large Scotch, despising himself for needing it. Then he unlocked a small safe in his bedroom, removed a few newspaper cuttings, and spread them over his bed. One, dated seven years back, mentioned the marriage of art historian David Fletcher to student Eve Drummond. Another, five years later, spoke of Fletcher's death and the heavy debts he had left his young widow.

Luke took up the most recent cutting from a magazine. It showed a woman in her mid-twenties, startlingly beautiful, with hair the color of rich honey. Her skin seemed to glow with life, and her full mouth was curved in a half smile that any man would have been glad to interpret as an invitation. Yet the smile was directed, not at a man, but at a small figurine that she held lovingly in her two hands, and which seemed to draw her into another world. She was clad in a dark dress that was austerely chic, with a simple elegance that only money could buy. The soft material clung to her figure, all the more provocative because she seemed unaware of the beauty of her body. Her hair was drawn back in a businesslike style. Its severity told one story while that smile told another. The contrast made her the eternal Eve, mysterious, unfathomable. The caption spoke of her as "rising young art expert, Eve Drummond," but didn't mention why she'd abandoned her late husband's name.

There were two snapshots, as well. Luke held one of them against the magazine cutting. It showed the same woman, but she might have been another person: Eve Drummond at sixteen, young, natural and adorable, her hair blowing freely in the wind, her eyes alight with merriment.

After some hesitation he lifted the other photograph. There was Eve again, with a young man whose arm was curved possessively around her waist. He was twenty-three, dark-haired, tall and strongly built. He'd had no scar then. His face had been handsome in a sturdy, blunt-featured way, a face to gladden a woman's heart, especially then, when it bore a look of such total adoration. He was oblivious of the camera. He saw only the girl he held close. Luke was hard put to recognize himself as he'd been ten years ago, boyish, happy, wildly in love.

But he, too, had been another person. In those days his name had been John Baxter and he'd lived and worked on the estate of Tyler Drummond. Tyler had built up a fortune from a company making food products and become the local grandee, wealthy, arrogant and impatient of those he considered fools. He'd cared for only one person on earth, his charming, willful granddaughter, Eve. And John Baxter, a laborer without a penny to his name, had dared to raise his eyes and love her.

One

The early part of John's life had been shaped by three women. There was Helen, his mother, widowed before he was born and dead the day of his birth. Then there was Megan, Helen's mother, who'd taken him back to Drummond Lea, the estate where she'd lived and worked all her life. He'd grown up there, part of a community of servants, gardeners and small tenant farmers, and yet not part of them. From the moment he could think clearly he'd known that one day he must be his own master.

Most of those years were lost in a blur, but some memories stood out sharply. There was Tyler Drummond himself, a big, harsh man in early middle age, with sharp blue eyes. The first time he met Tyler John felt those eyes burn into him, almost as though their owner were angry. He'd been only a child then, but he'd stared back defiantly, knowing this man was trying to intimidate him and refusing to let it happen. It was Tyler who looked away first. And

John's grandmother had given a sharp laugh that sounded like a crow of triumph and kissed him.

There was Antony, Tyler's mild-mannered son, and his only offspring. "Couldn't say boo to a goose," Megan had observed contemptuously, and Tyler had seemed to think so, too. Antony didn't live at Drummond Lea but visited occasionally, bringing his lovely wife, Caroline. Then they stopped visiting, and Megan said they'd gone to live abroad.

Tyler had lived alone in his great mansion, seemingly untroubled by his solitary state. "He cares for no one and no one cares for him," Megan had observed with a shrug.

After some years, his solitude was broken by Parry, his great-nephew, who attended boarding school in England while his parents worked in the Far East. For his vacations Parry came to Drummond Lea, and he and Luke were instantly antagonistic. Parry was a graceful, feline boy with cold eyes and a fey, delicate charm that he showed to those he considered worth the trouble. John despised him, and since he didn't bother to hide it, he earned Parry's dislike, which only made him laugh.

He was twenty-two in the summer when they first clashed, a genial young giant who'd taken over the working of Megan's rented plot and managed it single-handed. He'd sometimes see the boy out riding. Despite his delicacy and the fact that he was only fifteen, Parry handled Tyler's high-bred horses with skill and liked nothing better than to ride among his grandfather's tenants, looking down loftily from a Thoroughbred's back.

Once he reined in beside John, who was harvesting potatoes and putting them in a sack that rested on a bench. "Are they any good?" Parry demanded, pointing to the potatoes with his riding crop.

There was nothing very strange in the boy's interest. Tyler preferred to buy his produce from his own tenants, often conducting the sale personally so that he could beat down the price. But something in the way Parry was looking at him told John the potatoes were an excuse. "They're the best you'll find around here," he said quietly, holding one up.

Parry turned it over and shrugged. "Not really up to standard," he said, tossing the potato back. At the same moment he nudged the full sack with his toe so that its precarious balance was upset and potatoes tumbled out over the ground. Parry giggled. "Sorry."

"Pick them up," John said quietly.

Parry gave a derisive grin and tried to wheel his horse away, but John grasped the bridle and repeated, "Pick them up."

"Let go of my bridle," Parry snapped, his face flushing.

"When you've picked those potatoes up."

"Pick them up yourself." Parry tried to yank the horse's head free, but John stood there, immobile, holding the animal steady without apparent effort. Then he reached up to curl his free arm around Parry's waist and hauled him struggling to the ground.

"Pick them up," he repeated.

Parry's answer was to kick John hard on the shins. John gave no sign of pain but calmly removed the boy's riding crop, tucked him under his arm and applied the crop twice to his seat. "Now get to work," he ordered.

Parry's face was red with temper and humiliation. Tears streamed down his cheeks as he gathered up the potatoes and flung them into the sack. "I suppose that'll have to do," John said at last. "You're not used to work, are you? Pity."

"You won't get away with this," Parry screamed through his tears. "I'll tell my great-uncle."

John grinned. "Go ahead."

Parry cast him a look of loathing and galloped off, followed by the sound of John's laughter.

But Megan didn't laugh when he told her. "You want to be careful," she warned him.

"Of that pretty boy?" he scoffed.

"There's something about him that scares me," she admitted. "He's the kind that pulls insects' wings off for fun."

"He won't get far if he tries that with me," John pointed out. "Don't worry. He won't tell his grandfather that I walloped his rear."

"No, but he won't forgive you."

"Am I supposed to lose sleep over that?"

"Just you watch your back," Megan said, but he only laughed again. The next day they heard that Parry had departed to spend the last week of his vacation with friends.

John worked hard on Megan's land. But while his hands were busy his brain still seethed with dreams of another life. He started taking business courses at night school. Megan sighed and prophesied, "You'll leave me, just as she did."

"You mean my mother?" he asked in the gentle voice he used on the rare occasions when he spoke of Helen. The thought of the mother he'd never known was too sacred in his mind to be touched often by speech.

"She went away," Megan repeated, "and I never saw her again. You'll go, too. You're ... you're like her."

News came that Antony and Caroline had died in a car crash. If Tyler Drummond grieved for his son, he gave no sign of it, but he set off at once to collect their daughter and bring her to live at Drummond Lea.

And so Eve Drummond came into John's life, the third and most unforgettable of the women who'd made him what he was.

John made some spare cash doing carpentry, and when Tyler summoned him to the house to mend a chair, his only thought was that he was going to insist on a just price. But while he was at work the door opened and a girl with honey-colored hair and deep green eyes walked in, and in a moment his world was turned upside down.

She was in riding jodhpurs that clung revealingly to her slim thighs and hips. She had a woman's figure, but her face still bore the softness of a child. She smiled when she saw him, and the sun came out, filling the room with glory. "Hello, can you help me?" she asked cheerfully. "I can't get my riding boots off by myself."

She sat in one of the high leather chairs and pushed against his rear while he stood astride her leg, easing the boot off. When they changed over, he could feel the shape of her foot pressed against one taut buttock, and heat flooded through him.

She thanked him and jumped to her feet, going to stand by the high window and running her hands through her hair in the sunlight. She was spring. She was all joy and beauty bound up in one perfect creature, and he loved her from that moment.

He supposed they introduced themselves, but he could never remember the words, only her sweet smile and the warmth in her eyes, the red lips that enthralled him, and the husky voice with a slight catch in it that was like music.

That night Megan scolded him for leaving his food untouched, saying, "Your favorite steak and kidney pie that I made specially." He apologized hastily and escaped into the cool evening air where he could be alone to dream of Eve.

There was a small wood nearby. He wandered in and leaned against a tree with his eyes closed, thinking of her, wondering if he'd be tormented like this all his days and if there was any cure, but also knowing that he didn't want a cure even if there was one, that it was better to suffer forever than never to know this wonderful feeling. Then he

opened his eyes, and she was there. He thought she was part
of his dream and said, "I was waiting for you," before he
could stop himself.

"Did you know I'd come?" she asked, and he realized
that she was real and blushed like the boy he still was for
what he'd given away.

"No, no, I . . . was thinking of something else," he said
hastily. But her laugh told him she wasn't fooled.

"You forgot your hammer this morning," she said. "I
came to bring it back to you."

It might have been true. In the state he'd been in he could
have forgotten every tool he had. But when he looked into
her eyes he knew she'd taken the hammer to have an excuse
to seek him out. She'd known that he would be waiting for
her, just as he'd known she would come to him.

They walked together under the stars, boy and girl, in-
toxicated with each other. When he heard that she was only
sixteen, he was assailed by guilt. She was too young and
vulnerable for the mad desire that shook him whenever he
looked at her. Thoughts and images of the two of them together, naked limbs entwined, burned into his brain, but she
was little more than a child. He resolved never to meet her
again like this, never to go where he might accidentally en-
counter her. It would drive him to the edge of insanity, but
he'd endure it for her sake. Already his love held as much
tenderness as desire.

But when they said good-night she stood looking at him
wistfully, her lips slightly parted, and no power on earth
could have stopped him from taking her into his arms and
kissing her with all the force of his newly awakened passion. To his joy, he felt her desire surge up to meet his. She
kissed like a girl who had never kissed before, but under the
eager lessons of his mouth she learned quickly, letting her
lips part with a little sigh of bliss that went to his heart.

When they said a reluctant good-night, his conscience tormented him, making him groan as he lay awake in the small hours. This time he swore he'd be strong and avoid her.

But she wouldn't let him. She sought him out, desolate at his desertion. Her misery wrung his heart, and all the love he'd been fighting broke through and poured over her like a shower of gold. She gloried in it, lavishing her own passion on him in return.

The first time they made love he knew that life could hold nothing sweeter or lovelier. They met, as always, in a natural hollow in the wood, where the crowded trees provided some privacy. She pulled him down beside her on the ground, letting her fingers caress the back of his neck. "Eve, please," he begged.

"Don't you like that?" she asked mischievously.

"I like it too much. If you knew what it does to me . . ."

"Tell me what it does," she commanded, laughing.

But he shook his head, dumb with love and longing, knowing there were no words for what happened to him when he was with her, and that their union was as inevitable as the turning of the world upon its axis.

She was in shirt and jodhpurs, and when his shaking hands opened the buttons, he found she had nothing on underneath. Her eagerness to make love with him was the last straw that snapped his control, and in another moment he buried his face against the silky skin of her perfect breasts, inflamed past bearing. She moaned softly as he caressed the pink nipples with his tongue, moving her hands over him in a sensual discovery that delighted him and heightened his passion.

He parted her legs and moved over her gently, fighting to keep control for her sake. As soon as he entered her he knew he was her first man, but she had no hesitancy. Her hips moved instinctively in rhythm with his, and she looked up at him with shining eyes.

"Eve," he murmured, "my love . . . my only love . . ."

"Am I truly your love?" she pleaded.

"Always and forever."

It felt right to be a part of her, to feel her enfold him deep within herself. It was like coming home, and he knew that in all his life no other home would be as sweet. When he began to move faster she was ready for him, and they climaxed together, glorying in their perfect unity. Afterward she snuggled up to him blissfully. "I didn't think I could ever be as happy," she whispered.

Perhaps it was a presentiment that made him answer, "I wonder if we'll ever be so happy again."

"Of course we will," she said. "We'll be together all our lives, and we'll make love, and love each other, and love each other, and make love . . ." She trailed off into happy laughter.

Her fairy-tale vision of the future reminded him how recently she'd left childhood behind, and he tightened his arms protectively, wanting nothing more than to care for her forever. He'd have laid down his life for her. "I want to marry you," he whispered.

"Of course," she said at once, but her tone was vague.

"Don't you want to marry me?"

"Of course I do. But Grandpa will hit the roof if I tell him I want to marry at sixteen, and I don't want to fight with him. Let's just enjoy being happy."

He was disappointed but told himself to be patient. Their love would endure.

The rest of that summer they met whenever they could and loved each other with increasing ardor. When they lay in each other's arms, John felt they were truly one, heart and mind as well as flesh. Yet at other times he had a strange feeling that she'd gone beyond him.

Once he awoke from dozing with his head in her lap to find her making rapid strokes on a small sketching block she often carried with her. When he tried to raise his head, she said, "Don't move," in a voice that was almost sharp, and pushed him down again. When she let him up, he saw a charcoal sketch of himself. Despite its roughness it was good. She'd caught his essential quality, the massiveness in the neck and shoulder muscles, the uncompromising line of his jaw. But he scowled, sharply aware of her rich girl's elegance and feeling that she'd made him look like a farm laborer. When he said so she laughed, not unkindly, but with a complete lack of understanding.

Another time she appeared wearing a pendant with a colored stone, shaped like a beetle. "It's a scarab," she explained. "Like they wore in ancient Egypt. Of course it's only a reproduction. Grandpa bought it for me when we went to the British Museum."

"What made him drag you around a place like that?"

She chuckled. "He didn't. I dragged him. Poor Grandpa. He hated it. He said it was nothing but bones and stones. But I loved it. Everything's so old and beautiful and—your eyes are glazing just like his did."

"I'm not surprised. You actually think that beetle's beautiful?"

"It's a scarab," she corrected him firmly.

"All right, what's a scarab?"

"Well...it's a kind of beetle." She saw him grin and said quickly, "a *sacred* beetle. Oh, what's the use? You don't understand any more than Grandpa does."

A gap opened up between them, but they covered it with laughter and the mutual passion that was always there. As the summer wore on John hated the secrecy more and more, and longed only for the day he could claim her openly, but he felt he had to abide by her wishes.

Nevertheless, happiness made them careless. One day, walking with their arms entwined, absorbed in each other, they looked up to find her grandfather standing in their path. "Get off home," he ordered Eve.

But she stood her ground until John whispered, "Go on," and that infuriated Tyler more than anything. She took a few steps past him and looked back at John. Over the old man's shoulder he saw her shake her head urgently, telling him the time wasn't right to speak of their love.

"I told you to go," Tyler ordered, swinging around to her. When they were alone, he demanded furiously, "What the devil do you think you're doing?"

"Walking with my arm around a girl," John answered. "Any reason why I shouldn't?"

"Don't you take that tone with me," Tyler barked. "What you do with girls of your own kind, I don't know and I don't care, but let me find you touching my grand-daughter again and I'll make you sorry."

He was one of the few men tall enough to look John in the eye, and they stood there confronting each other, the old bull and the young bull, each tensing for the other's next move. "I wonder how you'll manage that?" John remarked.

It was the amusement in the younger man's voice that made Tyler strike him across the face. He drew back his arm for a second blow, but John's hand closed over his wrist and held him easily. At last he released him, and Tyler stepped back bellowing, "Don't forget what I've said. Stay away from her." His face was full of bitterness. They both knew the young bull had won.

That evening John described the incident to Megan. "It makes no difference," he said. "We love each other and we're going to get married."

"Good for you," Megan observed briefly. "Girls of your own kind, indeed! She's no better than you if the truth were known."

"What do you mean?" John demanded.

"I mean, she's no more a Drummond than I am."

"Course she is. She's Tyler's granddaughter."

"Hah! He thinks she is!"

"What are you getting at, Gran?"

"Her mother wasn't what she seemed. I had a cousin who worked for Caroline's family, and she told me that everyone knew Caroline was mad about one of the stable lads. And him with a wife! When she got pregnant she had to find a husband fast, and she picked Antony Tyler because he was too besotted with her to see straight, besides being a fool at the best of times."

"I don't believe it," John said, ransacking his childhood memories of the ethereal Caroline who'd once given him candy for running an errand. "Why, she looked like a madonna."

"They're the worst," Megan said with a coarse laugh. "Your Eve passes for a high and mighty Drummond, but she's a little bastard and don't you forget it."

"That's enough!" John said, raising his voice to the old woman for the first time. "Whatever she is makes no difference. We love each other. And don't you go spreading this story around and making her unhappy."

"All right, all right. Why should I tell? I haven't told all these years."

"Promise me," he persisted, for the thought of Eve being hurt was unendurable.

Megan promised and observed cynically, "So you think you're going to carry her off from under Tyler's nose?"

"That's just what I'm going to do."

The next day Eve slipped out to meet him again. Her grandfather had ordered her to stay away from John, but had taken no steps to restrain her. It wouldn't have occurred to Tyler that his orders might be disobeyed. "He gave me a terrible lecture about marrying someone of my own kind." Eve sighed. "He wants me to marry Parry eventually."

"That nasty little boy!" he exclaimed.

"He's not nasty. I'm very fond of him."

"How can you be?" he demanded in disgust.

"Well, I am." She was young enough to enjoy his jealousy and tease him by saying, "He won't always be a little boy and he's very good-looking."

They had their first quarrel. He was too much in love to have any sense of humor or to appreciate that she was testing her powers as innocently as a kitten sharpening its claws for the first time. Eve caught a glimpse of the black temper that he'd never let her see before, and her own temper rose to meet it. The kitten became a cat, and by the time she stormed out his feelings were thoroughly lacerated.

But she was back the next day, hurling herself contritely into his arms and kissing him a hundred times in a minute. "Grandpa's planning to send me to a finishing school in Switzerland in a few weeks," she said desperately. "I can't bear it if we have to be apart."

"We'll never be apart," he promised. "We'll get married."

She kissed him again joyfully, but the next moment she said, "He'll never consent."

"It doesn't matter. We'll go to Scotland. Up there you can marry without his consent at sixteen. Let's go now."

"John, I can't just run off like that," she said quickly.

"Why not? Eve, you do love me, don't you?"

"I love you with all my heart," she said fervently, "but there are reasons why I can't elope just now. Don't press me, John. I'll come as soon as I can, I promise."

He pleaded with her several times over the next few weeks, but her answer was always the same—"just a little longer." She was strangely ill at ease, but he refused to recognize why this might be and assured himself over and over that she loved him. Their passion was still lovely, tumultuous, but afterward he sometimes saw her looking at him with fearful eyes.

Autumn came and Parry returned from school for the half-term vacation. John encountered him once with Eve. They were painting together, easels side by side on a grassy slope overlooking a small lake. As John watched, Parry rose and went to stand behind Eve, his hands on her shoulders, while she explained something about her painting. Parry smiled as if in perfect comprehension and pointed. He seemed to be making a suggestion, and Eve nodded eagerly and began to make a change in the picture.

An anger that was mostly fear rose in John. The mysterious world of the artist, where Eve lived so easily, and where he knew he couldn't follow her, was open to Parry, too. They could slip away into a private world from which his big, clumsy self was excluded. At that moment Parry's slightly inane giggle reached him. He turned his back and stalked off. Neither of them had noticed him.

The next day he said to her urgently, "I don't want to wait any longer. It has to be now."

A strange faraway look came over her face. "All right," she said at last. "Tomorrow."

He tried to push out of his mind the memory of that disturbing look. If it had been anyone but Eve he'd have said she was calculating something. He managed to buy an old car, and they agreed to meet at night in their usual hollow in the wood. When the evening came John said anxiously, "Gran, are you sure you'll be all right? I wish you'd come, too. I don't want you here when he finds out."

"Hah! I wouldn't miss his face for all the world."

"You really hate him, don't you?"

For a moment Megan's face became very old and very tired. "Yes, I do," she said. "I hate him because he's a murderer."

He gave an embarrassed laugh. There was more emotion in Megan's face than he'd ever seen before, and it made him feel awkward. "You don't mean that literally?"

"As near as makes no odds. I'll tell you this—if you ever get the chance to hurt him, take it. He's a murderer and don't you ever forget that."

"Then it's not safe for you to stay behind."

"Yes, it is. He won't do anything against me. I can't explain why, but one day I'll tell you. Get going."

He parked the car just inside the wood and walked on until he reached the hollow. He was a few minutes late, and as he neared the place he called softly, "Eve."

There was no reply, but he thought he heard a twig crack. "Eve."

The twig cracked again in front of him. But at the same moment there was another noise behind him, and before he could turn around the first blow smashed into the side of his head. It was followed immediately by another blow and then another. He fought back as hard as he could, but it was pitch-dark and there were at least three men punching him with brass knuckles. After a while they got him onto the ground and began kicking him with studded boots. Every impact made a sickening noise that shuddered through his raw flesh, but over it he heard another noise—a high, inane giggle.

At last they left him there, motionless, covered in blood. He lay half conscious for hours, his mind a hollow in which the sound of that giggle reverberated, until at dawn a passerby found him and called an ambulance.

He awoke in the hospital with pain in every part of his body and a dressing over his left eye. The nurse showed him a large envelope that had been found clutched in his hands. He had to get her to open it and hold up the contents for him. They were small gifts he'd given to Eve, cheap things by Drummond standards, but given with passionate, tender love. As he looked at them he felt the bile in his throat.

"There's a note with them," the nurse said. "Shall I read it to you?"

"Hold it up so that I can see it," he said hoarsely.

"I don't think you should—"

"Do it."

He had to fight to focus his one good eye, but at last he could see well enough to recognize Eve's distinctive writing. There was only one line: *I guess we both made a mistake.*

He sent the nurse away and tried to think clearly, but one picture dominated his mind: Eve's face with its strange, calculating expression when she agreed to elope. It had puzzled him, but now everything was horribly clear. Eve had never meant to marry him. The love that had been so great on his side was nothing but a rich girl's lust on hers. She had a body made for love, and through him she'd discovered sensual pleasure, but now he'd served his purpose and she was ready to toss him aside.

She couldn't confide in Tyler, who'd have exploded with wrath at her disobedience. But Parry would help her, if she could only delay until he was home from school. So she'd put her lover off on vague pretexts until Parry had returned, his pockets overflowing with money to hire some of the local louts whose idea of fun was to batter a man senseless. And Parry had known just where to wait because Eve had told him of the trysting place.

It was Eve Drummond who'd taught John that he could love deeply, with his whole soul. Now, through Eve Drummond, he discovered the power to hate. The blasting force of his hate shook his battered frame, obliterating everything but the desire for revenge on Parry, but most of all on Eve, who'd betrayed him.

A policeman came to ask him questions. Did he have any enemies? Had he recognized his assailants? John said no to both questions. Even if he could have convinced anyone that a delicate-looking schoolboy had set thugs on him, he reserved vengeance for himself.

It was the next day before Megan came. She'd pictured him safely far away until someone had discovered his old car on the edge of the wood. As soon as she entered, her hands flew to her mouth. "Oh, my God," she whispered. "Oh, my God."

John hadn't given any thought to his looks until he saw her horror. "Is it very bad?" he whispered.

She controlled herself and said with a valiant effort, "Just a few bruises and—and, of course, your face is swollen—but it'll go down, and you'll be just like before."

"I'll never be like I was before," he said, not talking about his face. "Gran, have you seen her?"

Megan shook her head. "She's vanished."

"She was wise. But I'll find her when I'm ready."

Megan started to speak, but something strange seemed to be happening. Her mouth was twisted and only gibberish emerged. The harder she tried the more her face contorted until at last she gave a terrible wail. Her body jerked violently, and she slid onto the floor and lay there in convulsions. John frantically yanked the bellpull and a nurse came running in.

They took Megan away, and he lay in torment for hours until the nurse returned and said, "I'm afraid your grandmother has had a stroke. We're doing the best we can for her, but she's an old woman."

"I want to be with her," he croaked.

She helped him heave his tormented body into a wheelchair and pushed him along the corridor to Megan's bedside. His grandmother lay as stiff as a board, making no sign of recognition even when he took her hand.

There was a hand mirror on the table and in the long, quiet hours he spent with her he gained his first glimpse of himself. His face was a puffed-up mass of red and blue marks, his lips swollen and cut. He was unrecognizable as the handsome, laughing young man of only a few days ago. No wonder, he thought, the sight of him had made Megan collapse.

At last the figure on the bed stirred and made a sound that might have been his name. "Yes, Gran, I'm here," he said eagerly.

He could see her fighting madly to say something, but all that came out was a horrible gurgling croak. "It doesn't matter," he said, torn apart by her struggle. "Don't try to speak, Gran."

But she fought until the end, seeming to know how little time she had. She was still fighting when the breath left her body. John hadn't wept for himself, but he laid down his head on Megan's still form and sobbed.

He forced himself out of the hospital in time for her funeral. He knew, by then, that the sight in his left eye was impaired for good. But it didn't matter. All a man needed for revenge was one good eye and a heart full of hate. And he had both of those.

Megan had given him the only love he'd ever known. He had thought he'd found love with Eve, but she'd turned out to be false and cruel, like all the Drummonds. Now, as he stood by Megan's grave, he knew that love had gone out of his life forever.

After the funeral he stayed staring down into the grave, and when he lifted his head there was Tyler standing on the other side, watching him. His expression was uneasy and Luke guessed that Tyler suspected who had caused his injuries. "I knew you'd be here," the old man said. "I was afraid you'd refuse to see me, if I went to the hospital."

"You were right," John said shortly.

Tyler seemed abashed, something John had never seen before. But he had no pity for him. This was a Drummond, head of the family that had tortured him, and killed the old woman whose body lay between them. "I know what's in your mind," Tyler said. "You want justice. Well, I'm here to give it to you."

John pointed into the grave. "She collapsed when she saw the state I was left in. You want to give me justice? Bring her back."

"I can't do that, But perhaps five thousand pounds—"

John balled his fists. "If you weren't so old, I'd break you into pieces for daring to offer me money for her death," he said venomously.

"It's not just her. Your face... your eye—" A tremor seemed to cross his face. "Money is all I have," he finished wearily.

"It's not enough."

"Then tell me what would be."

"To see you and your family suffer. Let me tell you a joke, Tyler. You were so sure I wasn't good enough for your granddaughter, but she *isn't* your granddaughter. Her father wasn't a Drummond. He was some stable lad Caroline fancied."

He hurled the words at the old man and waited, with grim satisfaction, for the reaction. But Tyler disappointed him. Instead of being devastated he merely nodded wearily and said, "Dermott Wilshaw. Yes, I knew."

"You *knew*?"

"Of course I knew. I found out years ago. I didn't betray Caroline. Why should I?"

"She deceived your son."

Tyler shrugged. "If a man's fool enough to be taken in, that's his problem. I was fond of Caroline. And Eve was the only person I loved. I couldn't have harmed her."

"Even though she's not a Drummond?"

"She *is* a Drummond," Tyler said fiercely. "She's a Drummond because I say so. Enough of this. The offer's still open."

"I don't want your money. Get away from my grandmother's grave. You desecrate it."

Tyler's ruddy face seemed to pale. He turned and stalked away into the fading light, a stiff figure.

John had gone directly to the funeral from the hospital. Now he returned to Megan's cottage for the first time since he'd left it such a short time ago, so happy, so deluded. He found the place ransacked, and all of Eve's gifts and letters to him were gone.

In that moment the bitter pain inside him vanished and was replaced with a deadly freezing chill. He was glad of it because now he was stronger.

He picked up the phone and called Tyler. "The price of your clear conscience is ten thousand pounds," he informed the old man.

Tyler gave a bark of cynical laughter. "I knew it. Every man has his price."

"Just get me the money at once," John said, and put down the phone without waiting for an answer.

He'd sought the trivial revenge of hurling Eve's history in Tyler's face, and it had failed. But his true vengeance would be something else, something planned and well thought out, that would need a great deal of money. It might take a long time to accomplish, for it meant getting Parry and Eve under his control. But he could wait.

For the next ten years nothing mattered to him but his goal. He changed his name so that he could approach his quarry unnoticed. He used Tyler's money shrewdly, worked night and day to build up his business, learned all the tricks of a ruthless world and then taught the world some new ones. He diversified, bought new companies, stripped assets, became a millionaire many times over.

Tyler Drummond's wealth had been in the family firm. When Parry's gambling debts forced Tyler to go public, Luke, acting through nominees, began to buy up the company. By the time Tyler died Luke held a controlling interest and knew that his moment had come.

He was well informed about his enemies for, like a beast of prey waiting to spring, he'd never taken his eyes off them, no matter how distant they might have seemed. He knew that Parry's work as a stockbroker did not make him enough money to live in the lordly manner he enjoyed, and that the dividend from his Drummond shares was vital to him. He knew that Eve's husband had died massively in debt and that it was Tyler's wealth which had brought her the good things in life.

They'd never met again after the aborted elopement. Now she was coming to beg a favor from Luke Harmon. But it was John Baxter who was waiting for her.

Two

Luke heard the car draw up and discreetly parted the curtains an inch. He was only one floor above street level and had a clear view of the woman who got out of the sleek, silver sports car. He studied her, trying to recognize the girl he'd known. The hair that had once been soft and loose was drawn back, revealing the perfect lines of her small, elegant head.

As she approached the door, he could see that her walk had lost the coltishness he'd once found endearing. He drew back quickly as she pressed the bell. "Yes?" he answered over the intercom.

"Eve Drummond."

He pressed the switch that opened the outer door, then went to open the door to his apartment. By the time Eve had come up in the elevator, he'd retreated to stand in a patch of shadow, with his right side toward her. He saw her pause in the doorway. "Come in, Miss Drummond," he called.

She walked inside, searching for him, and stood directly in the light of the window. He'd known her as the embodiment of spring, but now she wore the colors of autumn, olive green, orange and yellow, in a dappled silk dress that swirled about her slender legs. She'd been charming, young and adorable. Now she was sophisticated, desirable and magnificent. "Mr. Harmon?" she called in the soft, husky voice that had once turned him to water.

He clenched his hands against that remembered sensation. "I'm here."

She turned, and a great stillness came over her. "I can't see you very well," she said uncertainly. "For a moment I thought..."

"What did you think?" he asked, stepping forward.

She went deadly pale. *"John,"* she whispered. "John."

"I don't know anyone of that name," he said. "I'm Luke Harmon."

She didn't seem to hear him. "John, what are you doing here? How can it be you?"

"My name is Luke Harmon," he repeated.

"Don't keep saying that!" she cried. "You're John Baxter. I know you are. Why do you torment me by pretending?"

"If you like, I'll agree that I was once John Baxter, but that was a long time ago."

"Ten years, four months and three days," she said, as if in a dream.

He drew in his breath sharply at her remembrance. "You have an excellent memory for trivial details," he said at last. "I doubt if I could be as accurate. To me that time is so distant that it might be a thousand years. We're both different people now, and surely this interview will be easier on both of us if we start afresh, as the strangers we are."

Her head went up and she smiled defiantly. "You're quite right. I've never believed in dragging the baggage of the past around with me." She shrugged and added lightly, "It weighs so much."

"How wise you are. May I get you a drink?"

"Dry sherry, please."

He poured it, and as he came close she saw his scarred left eye for the first time. Her hand flew to her mouth in an impulsive gesture. She checked it instinctively, but not before he'd seen the shock and horror in her eyes. He turned away from her. "Perhaps we should get down to business at once," he said coldly.

"I'm sorry," she stammered. "Please don't misunderstand—"

"I don't think I have. Won't you sit down, Miss Drummond?"

He indicated a seat and chose one for himself from which he could present his good side to her gaze. "You had something you wished to discuss with me?"

"I thought I knew what I was going to say, but now the words have gone out of my head," she said, looking at him. "I just want to know what happened to you, and how you came to be here. How *can* you be the Luke Harmon I've read about?"

He shrugged. "I don't read what the papers say about me."

"That you're one of the most powerful men in the financial world. They say you live like a recluse, never letting anyone take your photograph. How could I ever think it might be you?"

"Why should you? Why should either of us give the other a moment's thought? Could we get down to business now?"

She looked as if she'd have liked to go on, but Luke's expression of cool amusement seemed to daunt her. "Very well," she said. "Can you explain to me what's happening? Parry and I had no idea how matters would be when our grandfather died. The lawyers have explained it, but...it all seems too incredible."

"Tyler was forced to start selling stock several years ago."

"And he sold to *you*?"

"To my companies."

"Compan*ies*—plural. Did he know all the roads led back to the same company?"

"Not at the time. But two years ago he found that Harmon Enterprises owned more than fifty percent. Frankly, I don't think he cared."

"But did he know that Luke Harmon was *you*?" she persisted.

"No, we never met."

She jumped as though she couldn't bear to be still and began to move restlessly about the apartment. She had a feline grace that had once made his senses ache. Now he watched coolly as she paced up and down like a young lioness in a cage. He'd built the cage up slowly around her until now she was his, trapped by his control over the major part of her income, and therefore her life. He wondered if she'd discovered the bars yet.

"He wouldn't have let you take over Drummond Foods if he'd known who you were," she said.

"He might. I don't think he felt particularly protective about Parry."

"And me? Tyler would never have knowingly left me in this position."

Yes, he thought, she felt the cage closing in on her, but she was still fighting. "I'm not quite certain what your position is, Miss Drummond, but from your presence here I imagine the dividend forms a vital part of your income."

"It has its uses," she said stiffly.

"And you blame me for what's happened? But surely this can't come as a complete surprise? You must know your cousin's skill in getting rid of money quickly with nothing to show for it."

She flushed angrily at his tone. "He's been unlucky. He lost a lot in the recent stock market fall. So did a lot of people. I dare say you did, too."

He shrugged. "I lost something, yes, but I'd invested rather more wisely than I imagine he had. Besides, I'm not talking about his investments, but of his gambling, which is extensive."

"I don't think the cause is relevant. Can't you try to see what it means to Parry to lose an inheritance he'd thought would be his?"

"Are you suggesting that I stole the shares in Drummond Foods? I assure you I paid handsomely for them."

"I'm not talking about the shares. It's Drummond Lea—he'd always thought it would be his."

"I can't see why. Surely you were the most likely heir?"

"I—I didn't want it. Tyler knew that. There was no question of it coming to me."

"Which is no doubt why he felt free to sell it to Drummond Foods. As the head of the company, he gave himself a guarantee that he could occupy the property for his lifetime. When I obtained control, I honored that promise, but I'm not prepared to transfer it to Parry. The estate is a valuable property."

"Yes, it could make you a fortune as an hotel or a conference center," she flashed. "Drummond Lea was a *home*."

He gave a cynical laugh. "I wonder how long it would have remained a home if your cousin had inherited it. He'd have lost no time selling it to the highest bidder."

"Parry isn't a spendthrift," Eve insisted. "It's just that this has happened so suddenly. Neither of us had any warning that our income was to be shut off overnight. You *can't* just leave us stranded like this."

"This really isn't a matter of personalities. *I'm* not leaving you stranded."

"Aren't you? Wasn't it you who refused to declare a dividend?"

"Yes, because in my opinion the firm can't afford one."

"That's nonsense," she declared flatly. "Drummonds has always been a profitable firm and declared handsome dividends."

"And why? Because Tyler paid out money that should have been ploughed back into the firm. It's far too long since any new machinery was installed. I'm planning an extensive program of modernization that will absorb profits for the next two years. After that, however, things will look up."

"And what do Parry and I live on in the meantime?" she demanded.

"I understood you were building a reputation in the art world."

"I do some free-lance scouting for art dealers on my travels. It doesn't pay all that much."

"I'm sure it doesn't keep up the standard of living you're used to. I sympathize, but I can't be responsible for the circumstances of every shareholder in my companies. I'm sorry, but my mind is made up."

"I can't believe that you could ever talk like this...not to me," she said slowly. "I know what happened was a long time ago and it ended badly but—"

"Badly?" He turned his face full toward her, and she saw the scar standing out against his livid face. He got hastily to his feet and poured himself a whisky, which he downed in

one gulp. "You'd better stop right there," he said harshly. "Let me warn you against using those memories. They won't move me. Quite the reverse."

Eve rose and stared at him.

"What am I supposed to remember, Miss Drummond? A romantic boy-and-girl idyll? I'm afraid my recollections are rather more prosaic. They include your grandfather, the 'grand old man' of the district, using his position to exploit and underpay anyone on his land, insulting his tenants with impunity because he had power. Tyler taught me the most valuable lesson I ever had—only power counts."

"Is that all you remember?" she asked. She was very pale.

"It's all I choose to remember," he said coldly. "It's better that way. Only the present matters."

For a moment he saw something on her face that amazed him. It was a withered, despairing look that reminded him startlingly of Tyler's face when they'd last met over Megan's grave. It lay incongruously on the young, beautiful features. He pushed the thought away. It was a weakness.

Eve put out a hand to him. "John—Luke, I know what you must think of me, but there were reasons for what I did."

He ignored her gesture. "Of course. Excellent reasons, no doubt."

"I did you a great wrong. I never meant to. It seemed harmless at the time, but afterward—"

"Do we really need to go into this? The wrong is in the past along with everything else."

"But how can it be when you don't even know—or do you? Did Tyler see you afterward? Did he tell you what I'd done?"

"Tyler and I had a very interesting conversation over my grandmother's grave. It was short and to the point. He offered me five thousand pounds compensation."

"Money? He dared to offer you money, as though that could compensate for anything?" Her face was young again and full of indignation.

"I thought so myself..." Luke began.

"So you hurled the offer back at him and told him what he could do with his money?" she supplied eagerly.

Luke regarded her curiously. "Did he never tell you about this?"

"He didn't even tell me he'd spoken to you."

"How curious."

"But if you flung it back at him, I don't suppose he'd want to tell me." Some quality in the silence that followed caught her attention because she asked uncertainly, "You *did* fling it back at him, didn't you?"

For a moment he would have given anything to be able to say yes. Instead he allowed his eyes to wander around his luxurious apartment, then looked back at her sardonically. She drew in her breath sharply.

"Aren't you being a little naive?" he asked wryly. "Where do you imagine all this came from? I had to get a start somewhere."

"You...took Tyler's five thousand pounds?"

"Not five...ten. I told him that was my price."

She paled. "I don't believe that."

He looked surprised. "Why not? You wrote me that we'd both made a mistake, but *I* didn't make any mistakes. Tyler Drummond's granddaughter came ticketed at a high price. I was very pleased with my bargain."

He told himself that here was the first part of his revenge: now she knew she'd been valued at hard cash, and that from her price had grown the power that had made her

prisoner in the hands of the man who hated her. But as he
watched the pain and disillusion in her face, he felt like a
shabby betrayer.

The feeling made him furious, and fury made him cruel.
"I'm sorry if you felt the figure should have been higher,"
he said coolly. "I pushed it as far as the market would take."

Eve turned swiftly away from him to the window and
stood staring into the street with blind eyes. Not for the
world would she have let this hard stranger see her now and
guess that his words had been like a blow in the face. Once
she could have told him every thought and feeling, but that
was a long time ago, and he had cruelly dismissed those bittersweet memories.

Suddenly her head went up. Very well then. If he wanted
to fight rough, he would discover that she could do the
same. She turned back and gave the brave, uncaring laugh
he'd heard her give once when her horse had thrown her and
she'd been in agony from a wrenched shoulder. "I'm sure
you got the last penny out of me," she said. "Well, I'm glad
you gained something out of that business. You've been on
my conscience—not very much, I must admit. But just a
little."

He gave a cold, deadly smile that didn't reach his eyes.
"And now I shall be there no longer. That's good. So it
looks as if we both came out of it with some profit. I trust
you found the experience useful?"

"Immensely." She considered him, her head to one side,
a provocative little smile playing around her lips, and spoke
with deliberate daring. "A woman should always choose her
first lover with care. I knew the day we met that you would
be strong. I had to take a chance on your being skillful as
well, but you were *very* skillful." She made her voice caress
the words. "Of course I didn't realize just how good you'd
been until later when I was able to make comparisons."

Sweat stood out on his forehead. "I'm flattered," managed to say.

She chuckled. "Well, don't be too flattered. I said y were good, but not incomparable."

Damn her for tormenting me, he thought.

"I find it hard to believe that your husband outpe formed me," he observed, "going by how much older th you he was."

It was a calculated risk. She knew now that he'd be watching her. But Luke was adept at knowing when to sa rifice a pawn. "I hope he left you well provided for," added, although he knew the answer.

Eve gave a little shrug and spoke lightly. "David left on debts. I had to sell our house to pay them. Since then I' got back onto an even keel, but only because of my Drui monds money. And I still don't have my own house."

"But the apartment you rent is in one of the most lux rious blocks in London," he observed.

"Yes, I have expensive tastes," she said defiantly. "I li quality."

"And you're a woman who should always have the be because you set it off so well," he said, nodding. "But t best costs."

"I've always been able to finance my life from n Drummonds dividends. Can't you see how unfair it is to c them off without warning? If you could start your moder ization program next year, Parry and I would have time adjust—"

"I'm afraid that wouldn't suit my plans."

"But surely your plans could be changed?"

"Any plan can be changed," he agreed.

"Well, then—"

"But only if the reason is good enough. I've placed orders for a lot of new machinery. To cancel now would cost me. The question is, can you make it worth my while?"

"How can I? If I had any ready cash, this conversation wouldn't be taking place."

"A beautiful woman doesn't need money to persuade a man," he drawled, looking at her. "I'm asking how far you'd be prepared to go."

She looked at him uncertainly. "I think I must have misunderstood you."

"You haven't misunderstood." He reached out and brushed his fingers down her cheek. His face was a stone mask that betrayed none of the electric excitement of touching her skin. "I think you could be very persuasive," he mused softly, "if you went about it the right way."

Eve stilled herself against the treacherous thumping of her heart. She looked up into his face for a long moment. "You can go to hell," she said deliberately.

He laughed. "You do 'outraged virtue' very well. It might almost be genuine." He let his hand drift lower.

His blurred left eye only just saw her hand drawn back ready to slap his face. He tensed, refused to duck the blow, but it never landed. At the last minute she checked herself, her eyes on the scar, and her hand flew to her mouth as she realized what she'd been about to do.

Rage, bitter as bile, rose and choked him. She wouldn't strike his damaged face, and her very restraint was an insult. "What's stopping you?" he grated. He seized her hand and drew it, resisting, up to the scar. "Hit me if you want to."

"I can't," she cried, snatching her hand away.

"Why not?" he snapped. "Because it would disgust you to touch me? Because to you I'm some kind of cripple that has to be protected. Damn you, how *dare* you pity me!"

"I don't—for God's sake stop this!"

"You'd have struck any other man, wouldn't you have' But not me, because I'm disfigured and you think tha makes me less than a man."

"That's not true—"

"I was man enough for you once, man enough to mak you a woman in my arms. You didn't flinch away from m in disgust then—"

"I didn't . . . it isn't . . . Listen to me—"

"But you've forgotten what that was like, haven't you You look at my face and you don't want to remember ho we were together, how you used to plead with me to love yo again . . . and again. You weren't merely willing, you wer eager, and you'd hate to think I could still make you feel lik that."

The sudden look of horror on her face inflamed him lik a match to a touchpaper. He reached out and pulled he hard against him. With a swift movement he tugged at he severely arranged hair so that it was released and cascade down about her shoulders in the old way. He twined hi fingers into its luxurious thickness, pulling her head back s that he could see her face. With her hair flowing free, sh looked so much like the girl he'd loved that a wild, an guished feeling swept through him, and he lowered hi mouth to hers in the first kiss since the last time they'd sai goodbye.

Her mouth was as sweet as forbidden fruit, softly shape for enticement, and the feel of it against his drove him wild He'd held other women in his arms over the years. Some ha frankly offered themselves in return for his money, other had been fond of him or would have been if he'd let them ge that close to his heart. But he never had. He'd traded lust fo cash, paid his debts scrupulously and forgotten them.

But this woman was different. She'd had the best of him
in the days when there was still a best to be had. She'd had
his only true love and his young, innocent passion, and
he'd destroyed them as casually as she'd have snuffed out
a light. Now the wheel had turned full circle and she was his
to destroy in turn if he wanted, or perhaps to enjoy. And he
discovered that hate was as potent as desire, flaming along
his nerves, turning him to pure sensation.

After the first moment's shocked rigidity, Eve began to
struggle, twisting her head away from his seeking lips.
"No," she protested. "John . . . you mustn't—"

"Those days are past," he growled. "Nobody tells me
now what I must and mustn't do. I do what pleases me, and
his pleases me."

He covered her mouth again quickly, feeling her lips close
against him. He began to work on them skillfully, tracing
their generous outline with his tongue, feeling her beginning to tremble. He murmured against her mouth, "Once I
made myself your slave. I believed in love and the pretty
fairy tales, and I'd have lain down and died for you. Do you
remember that?"

"Yes," she whispered.

"But you taught me better. You showed me that this is all
there really is—"

"That's not true—"

He gave a harsh laugh. "It's true all right. Once that lesson's been learned it can't be unlearned. Suppose I told you
that you could wipe out all debts if you went about it the
right way?"

"Not that way—no, John."

He slipped his tongue into her mouth and tightened his
arms so that she was pulled against his big, hard body.
Suddenly she relaxed against him, no longer fighting but not
accepting him, either. Her mute defiance maddened him,

and he drove his tongue harder into her, trying to force her into surrender, or at least the admission of his power over her. She owed him that.

As a girl she'd carried the scents of spring, wild thyme and sunshine. The woman was pervaded by the aroma of musk and heat, tormenting him with hints of unspoken secrets. Once he'd deluded himself that she belonged to him. Now he knew that the years had made her more elusive still. He might revenge himself on her and still find that she'd slipped through his fingers. He was shaken by a mad desire to possess her, to make her acknowledge the past's hold on the present, to acknowledge *him*.

He drew back and looked down into her face, finding there not the fear he'd half expected but an unbearable sadness. "You're right," she said. "You're a different man. John Baxter would never have kissed me like that. It would have been better if I'd never met Luke Harmon."

"But you were always bound to meet him," he said, not releasing her. "Haven't you realized that yet?"

Her eyes widened. "You planned this? You set out to get the firm—"

"I set out to get *you*. What do I care about the damn firm? I laid my traps years ago and waited for you to walk in. And now you're here, where I always meant you to be."

"In your power you mean?" she flashed. "You said only power counted—oh, I don't believe this is happening."

"Believe it. We have a score to settle, Eve, and this time the power's on my side."

She read the truth in his bitter face and whispered, "What kind of devil have you become?"

"The kind I was taught to be by you and your family. I've learned your lessons well. No mercy. No pity. Don't get mad, get even. You may recognize Tyler's philosophy."

"Oh, yes," she said with a bitterness that startled him. "I recognize Tyler's philosophy."

"You never thought you'd meet me again, did you, Eve? But you should have realized that there was bound to be a reckoning for what you did."

Before she could answer he pulled her against him and kissed her fiercely again. He wondered if the tremors he felt going through her were distaste at his scarred face or the echoes of an old desire like that which had started in him. He could tell through her clothes that this was still the beautiful body he'd once held. It had been designed to enslave a man, and the years hadn't made him immune to its spell. The old madness began to flame through him, and suddenly he felt her move against him, not fighting him but sliding her hands up until she could caress him with skilled fingers. Her lips were moving against his, seducing him with promises of infinite delight, such as he hadn't known since she'd left him. She was still the only woman who could make him feel as though nothing mattered except to make love with her and revel in the sensual richness of her body. A man might count the world well lost if he could only possess this one woman....

With a sudden jolt he came back to himself, and he was assailed by fear. He'd been so sure of himself, yet already he was succumbing to her dangerous magic, ready to become her victim again.

At the same moment she pulled back from him, struggling frantically to free herself. She was wild-eyed and breathing quickly, as though in the grip of a fear as great as his own. "No," she panted. *"Let me go."*

He had a last look at her face, full of horror, before she wrenched herself out of his arms and fled.

Three

——

Parry Drummond lived in a delightful mews residence that he'd designed and decorated himself. It was a tiny house filled with delicate objets d'art, but Parry's obsessive neatness prevented it from seeming cluttered, and none of the lovingly collected artifacts were as perfect a piece of workmanship as Parry himself.

The pretty boy had grown into a beautiful young man, tall and fair, with a willowy elegance that sent his tailor into ecstasies. His blue eyes were large and candid, his smile charming, and he was always in demand socially, for not everyone detected the faint chill that emanated from him. Eve had rarely detected it and then only faintly, partly because her constant traveling had prevented her from being in Parry's company for long, and partly because he always showed her his best side.

She hurried to see him as soon as she left Luke. He was watching for her and pulled open the front door, bestowing a light kiss on her cheek. "What's up, darling?" he asked, taking her coat. "Tell me the worst."

"Parry, something terrible has happened. I've just seen John Baxter."

He frowned. "What are you talking about?"

"John Baxter. Don't you remember him—from Drummond Lea?"

"Good grief, you don't mean the gardener's boy, do you?"

"He wasn't the gardener's boy. He rented a smallholding from Tyler."

"Well, whatever. He was a horny-handed son of the soil."

"Don't talk about him like that," Eve said fiercely.

"Sorry, pet. I didn't mean to offend you."

"Parry, listen to me. John Baxter *is* Luke Harmon."

"How can he be?"

"He changed his name and went into business, and now he's running our firm."

Parry was still for a moment, his smile fixed rigidly on his face. "That's impossible," he said at last.

"I've just seen him, and it's the same man, only he calls himself Luke Harmon now." She pressed her hands against her flushed cheeks. "I used to be in love with him."

"Yes, I remember you telling me when we were kids. But that was a teenage infatuation. You went away and got over it, didn't you?"

Memories of Luke's lips burning hers with bitter passion, and her own overwhelming response rose up in Eve, making her momentarily dizzy. She turned quickly away from Parry, afraid that her face might reveal feelings so private and shocking that she couldn't share them even with him. "I wanted to marry him," she said at last, "but Tyler made me jilt him in the most cruel way, and then packed me off to Switzerland. I never saw him again—'' her eyes were wild ''—until today.''

''Didn't you write to him?''

''Only the one letter breaking it off, and that was a horrible, cold note because Tyler made me write to his dictation. In reply he returned everything I'd ever given him, and all my letters with 'Bitch' scrawled over them. Tyler sent them on to me.''

Parry frowned. ''That was a rough thing for the old man to do, wasn't it?''

''I suppose he wanted me to understand that it was really over. And yet, if that's true, it's strange that he never told me John had taken a ten-thousand-pound payoff.''

''*What?*''

''That's how he built his fortune.''

Parry gave a low whistle. ''What's he like now?''

''Horribly changed. He's harder and he's got a scar over his left eye that looks as if it came from a nasty injury.''

Parry seemed absorbed in his drink. ''Did he tell you how he got it?'' he asked casually.

''No, I couldn't get through to him. Oh, Parry, we loved each other so much, and now he's become cold and cruel and . . . vengeful.''

''What do you mean?'' he demanded quickly.

''He hates me for what happened. That's really why he wanted Drummonds—because of me.''

''He actually said that?'

''Something like that. I'm not sure of the exact words, I'm so confused.''

''And the dividend?''

''We can forget that. He won't budge.'' She placed a hand on his arm. ''I'm sorry. Do you need the money very badly?''

''Yes, very. Evie, this could be serious.''

"Have you been gambling again, or what?"

Out of sight Parry ground his nails into his palm. Gambling didn't begin to describe it. "Or what," he agreed evasively.

She sighed and ruffled his hair. "Silly boy," she chided.

"Never mind. Something will turn up." He looked at her agitated face and said gently, "It's given you a nasty turn, meeting him like that, hasn't it?"

She nodded.

"Still keen on him?"

"No," she said vehemently. "That was over long ago. Please, Parry, I . . . I don't want to talk about it."

"All right, darling, don't get upset. Let me fetch you a drink."

While Parry was at the liquor cabinet the doorbell rang. Eve went to answer and found a motorcyclist standing there. "Special delivery for Mr. Parry Drummond," he said, holding out an envelope.

"I'll take it."

"You wouldn't be Eve Drummond, would you?"

"I would."

"Then here's one for you, too. Mr. Harmon said I'd probably find you here. Good night."

Eve tore open her envelope and read:

Luke Harmon requests the pleasure of Miss Drummond's company next weekend at Drummond Lea to meet a few friends and review the current situation.

"Cheek!" she exploded. She handed Parry his envelope. "How dare he!"

But Parry's brow cleared as he read his invitation. "To review the situation," he repeated. "That sounds promising. Not that I much fancy being invited to my old home, but beggars can't be choosers.''

"He must have sent these off as soon as I left," Eve fumed, "and he even told the messenger he'd find me here. He was so sure I'd come straight over to you."

"Well, you did."

"That's not the point. He understands too much. He knew all about me. He must have been keeping tabs. I thought I knew him once, but now there's something scary about him."

"Nonsense. You're imagining things. This is our chance to change his mind. Our only real problem is that he's mad at you for jilting him, although he seems to have made a very good thing out of his payoff. I'm sure you could 'take care' of him if you put your mind to it, couldn't you, my pet?"

"Parry, if you mean what I think you do, you can forget it," Eve said fiercely. "I just couldn't do that."

"Of course you couldn't," he said immediately, at his most charming. "What a beast I was to suggest it."

But Parry was far from being as calm as he appeared. Life, in his view, hadn't been fair to him, and most of his misfortunes stemmed from John Baxter, a man he'd loathed on sight. It had been a pleasure to be able to put his loathing into tangible form, but he'd paid dearly for it. Tyler had heard of Baxter's injuries and begun to look strangely at Parry. But he'd asked no questions, perhaps fearing the answers. Nor had he, apparently, mentioned his suspicions to Eve, but he'd never again spoken of marriage between them.

That was a pity. Eve had been the old man's favorite, and doubtless the cash would have flowed more freely after the wedding. Instead, he'd had to make do with a beggarly ten percent of the firm while Eve had been given thirty. He'd had to go into stockbroking, where his flair and facility had brought him a certain success, though it hadn't feathered his nest as handsomely as he'd hoped. He had a lot to blame John Baxter for.

Now this man, of all men, held Parry's fate in his hands. But he had no choice except to bluff it out. There was no proof. It had been a dark night, and Baxter was more likely to suspect Tyler than anyone else.

"All I ask," he said to Eve, "is that you accept this invitation. We'll go together and you can smooth my way a little. I'll do the rest."

"All right. I can't refuse you that. But you do the talking."

"I suppose you've got to admire him for having got this far," Parry mused. "But the seeds were always there."

"What do you mean?"

"He was very much a dictator even when he was no more than a laborer. We had a brush once, which I admit was mostly my fault. He was harvesting his potatoes and I knocked the sack over. It was sheer accident, and I'd have been glad to help him pick them up if he hadn't ordered me to. But once he started barking at me like a sergeant major, I got stubborn and told him to pick up his own potatoes." He gave a rueful smile. "I was an appalling brat at fifteen."

She smiled back. "What happened?"

"He hauled me off my horse and used my own riding crop on me."

Eve's smile vanished. "He beat you with a whip, a fifteen-year-old boy? That's horrible."

"There was always a touch of the brute about him, darling. He kept it hidden from you, but the rest of us knew. Well, he can lord it over us now, and I suppose he's enjoying it."

"Yes," Eve said slowly. "I have a feeling you're right. Parry... I'm afraid."

"Nonsense. Our luck's turned. Now let's forget it. I want to show you what I bought today."

"Shouldn't you be saving money?"

"The little I could save is a drop in the ocean compared to what I need. Besides, I'm sure this is worth far more than the thousand I paid."

He produced a small oil painting, and Eve studied it carefully before shaking her head regretfully. "If I were you, I should sell it straight back," she advised. "That is, if the buyer will take it. He's probably relieved to have got rid of it for as much as a thousand." She looked at Parry's defeated face and felt again how tenderly she loved this cousin who was more like a brother. How well they understood each other! No one else had ever been so perfectly on her wavelength, not Tyler, who had adored her in his blunt, blinkered fashion. Not even John...

She caught herself up with a sharp intake of breath that made Parry stare at her. "Don't take my word for it," she said quickly. "I can have it valued by someone else."

"No point," Parry said with a shrug. "When you give it the thumbs-down, that's it." He grinned and added amiably, "Why can't you have the decency to be wrong sometimes?"

"It's just a pity I'm not as bright about men as I am about pictures," she observed with a sigh. "Goodbye, love. I'll see you on the weekend."

She kissed his cheek and vanished. Parry went to the window and watched her get into her car, his face twisted into a wry smile. There'd been an irony about her last remark, which Eve—dear, innocent, straightforward Eve—had totally failed to appreciate. But he'd discerned it, as he discerned everything that could be turned to his advantage.

He stood at the window long after she had disappeared. He was very thoughtful.

Instead of returning to her hotel Eve headed her car north and drove until she was almost on the outskirts of London. She parked in a side street and began to walk. She moved automatically, her head reeling with what had happened tonight. Only a little while ago her world had seemed peaceful, if not actually happy. It had been years since she'd asked herself if she was happy. By the early age of twenty she'd learned to settle for peace as a compromise, and it had worked until tonight, when a grim ghost had risen from her past, threatening vengeance.

She wondered what he'd say if she told him that he'd had his vengeance a thousand times over in the years since their last meeting. He'd had it in every tortured, lonely night she'd endured and in every cry from a heart broken by the burden of the harm she'd done him. He'd haunted and destroyed her as finally as she'd destroyed him, and now he had come back to tell her that she must pay. It was almost funny.

She found that her feet brought her to a tiny antique shop where she occasionally picked up oddities. Although it was late, the lights were on and she could see the elderly owner pottering about. She waved to him and he let her in.

"I'm afraid I've got nothing that would interest you at the moment," he said, "but come in for a cup of tea."

Eve followed him into his tiny back room, which was a shambles, its shelves packed with items still waiting to be dealt with. Almost at once a tiny porcelain figurine of a man in eighteenth-century costume caught her eye.

She took it between loving fingers and examined it with breathless delight. When she turned it over she found what she'd expected, the trademark of crossed swords that meant she was holding genuine Meissen. Of course, that trademark could be faked, but knowledge born of love seemed to stream from the porcelain, through her skin, up into her brain and heart, telling her that this was the real thing. "It's exquisite," she said softly.

"But not perfect, unfortunately," he said. "Look." He indicated a chip on the little man's heel. "Such a tiny flaw, but it's enough to spoil the whole thing. I was about to smash it."

"No, you mustn't," she said quickly, holding the figure to her protectively. "It's still beautiful. If it's positioned carefully you couldn't see that chip."

"But it's worthless."

Eve shook her head. "Only in terms of money."

The old man grinned. "Now you're being sentimental."

"Perhaps I am, but I can't bear to think of throwing away something that's still lovely just because it has one little imperfection."

"That's all it takes to ruin an antique," he said with a shrug.

"But Meissen didn't set out to manufacture 'antiques'," she objected. "They were trying to create beautiful things that would give people pleasure. And there's so little beauty in the world that it doesn't feel right to destroy any of it, even if it's flawed. After all, you don't throw away people you're fond of just because they have faults."

"That's different. I've never found a person yet that was worth what that would cost if it was perfect," he said cynically. She laughed and he added, "You can have it if you like. Just take it out of my sight."

She hurried back to her car with the figure, laid it carefully on the back seat and drove home. As she entered the luxurious apartment block where she lived she glanced upward, wondering how much longer she could afford to live

there. Then the thought passed as she remembered her new
treasure and she went quickly upstairs.

She unwrapped the little man and held him up carefully.
He was delightful. His plump face was still as perfect as the
day he was made and it seemed to her that he wore an apol-
ogetic look, as though asking her to pardon his regrettable
lapse.

He was over two hundred years old, yet the love and skill
that had made him were timeless. Perhaps, when he was
new, some other woman had been charmed by him, as Eve
was now. Unconsciously she began to smile, and as she did
so she felt her peace return. She'd left Parry's home with the
oppressive feeling that both he and Luke were just behind
her, hounding her. Now they melted away, taking with them
the pain and anger, leaving her alone with timeless beauty,
the only thing that had never failed her.

Drummond Lea was an ideal place for entertaining, a
huge, comfortable red brick mansion set in leafy acres. The
grounds had become overgrown in Tyler's last years, but
Luke had had the foliage cut back, revealing the beauty of
the original landscaping.

The house had been thoroughly cleaned from roof to
basement, and now the brass shone and the oak paneling
gleamed. Mrs. Carter, Luke's housekeeper, had dropped
hopeful hints about redecorating, but he'd refused. Apart
from some new rugs everything looked exactly as it had
when he'd been an estate worker, allowed into the house
through the back door and cautioned to wipe his boots.

He'd inspected the house, seeking a bedroom for himself
and rejecting all the grandiose apartments. At last his choice
had lighted on a small room sparsely furnished with old-
fashioned pieces of solid oak and a hard, narrow bed. It was
an incongruous choice for the master of the house, but

something about it appealed to him more than the suffocating plushness he found elsewhere. He said so to Mrs. Carter, and her reply gave him a disconcerted feeling.

"Aye, that's what Mr. Drummond always said. He slept in this room."

"*This* was Tyler's room?" Luke echoed, amazed.

"He wouldn't sleep anywhere else."

So he and Tyler had something in common. The idea gave him some sardonic amusement.

The one change he'd meant to carry out was the removal of Tyler's portrait from its position of honor above the carved fireplace in the living room, but for some reason he'd delayed giving the order.

The artist had managed to capture Tyler's essence on canvas. There was the massive, bullnecked man, his hair grayer and more grizzled than Luke remembered, but his eyes were the same, a startling blue that seemed to pierce anyone who tried to look into them. They were cold eyes, saying that here was a man who could size anyone up in a glance and contemptuously dismiss all but a very few. The man behind them would ride roughshod over whoever got in his way. It was impossible to imagine those eyes softening in tenderness.

The mouth was intriguing. Nature had given it sensual lines that were still evident near the end of his life, and yet it had a strangely withered look, as though bearing the legacy of a suffering that even Tyler had been unable to deny.

Luke wasn't a fanciful man, but he had the disquieting feeling that Tyler's gaze sometimes followed him, full of a mysterious communication. He tried to shake off the impression, but the night of the dinner party Tyler was still there.

He stared back defiantly, thinking, *So be it!* This was his night of triumph, only spoiled by the fact that Tyler had gone beyond his reach. Let him hang there, his painted eyes looking down on Luke's revenge. "Wherever you are," he murmured, "I hope you can see me."

He'd told Mrs. Carter to give Eve her own old room, but he hadn't visited it himself. Now, as he waited for his guests, he yielded to an impulse to see the place where she'd lived and dreamed and planned her betrayal of him. It was the best bedroom in the house and boasted a four-poster bed hung with white and lavender curtains. It was well lit, being on a corner, and he went to one of the large windows to look out at the stone terrace below and the grounds beyond.

Once he'd come to the terrace at midnight, drawn to her by irresistible love. He'd stood down there silently, content just to know she was near. Then she'd opened the window and seen him, and in another moment she'd slipped out of the house and they were in each other's arms. He turned away from the window and left the room abruptly.

He hadn't slept well since he'd met Eve again. She haunted his dreams, often causing him to awake, shaking. Last night he hadn't slept at all, yet he wasn't tired. Tension and the feverish activity in his brain buoyed him, making him feel light-headed and sharply aware of impressions, as though his nerves had lost a protective coating.

The sound of a horn outside told him the first guests had arrived. There would be thirty people here this weekend—business colleagues, a few rivals and one outright enemy. There were some with whom he was on friendly terms, but none of them were actual friends.

He went outside to greet them, and for the next hour he was the perfect host, ushering them inside, receiving their congratulations on his new home, ordering servants to show them their rooms. And all the time his ears were sharpened for the sound of her arrival.

At last everyone was there except Eve and Parry. The guests were all gathered in the drawing room having drinks and exchanging polite nothings until it was time to go up-stairs and change for dinner. Tension was rising in Luke at the thought that she might not come. The conversation about him suddenly seemed unusually vapid and tinny. A gray light hung over the scene, and a terrible sense of futility made him feel weary.

Then he heard the sound of a car on the gravel outside, and he had to set down his drink sharply because his hand was trembling. "Excuse me," he said abruptly, and went out into the hall.

Eve had just come through the front door, and stood looking about her uncertainly. With the strange heightened awareness that had come over him Luke realized she was sensing the atmosphere as he'd once seen a deer do when emerging into dangerous open country. Then she saw him, and it seemed to him that she shrank a little. He gritted his teeth and walked up to her. "I'm so glad you were able to accept my invitation," he said smoothly.

"Wouldn't have missed it for the world" came Parry's languid voice. He'd entered behind Eve.

Luke smiled and extended his hand to Parry, showing none of the revulsion he felt. "Drummond," he said heart-ily, "good of you to come."

He seized Parry's smooth, perfectly manicured hand in a vigorous shake, and he could feel the other man's over-whelming relief at this apparently friendly greeting. It was the relief of a cornered rat who'd seen an escape after all. It suited Luke to keep him off guard.

"I'm sorry we're late," Eve said in a low voice. She was looking at a point just over his shoulder.

"It doesn't matter, now that you're here," Luke assured her. He saw her glancing around the hall. "I haven't altered anything, Miss Drummond. Why don't you let me take you for a stroll on the grounds. I'm sure you're anxious to see the old places again."

Parry started to say, "Good idea, Evie," just as she shook her head.

"Thank you, but another time," she said hurriedly, moving toward the stairs. "I'm a little tired just now."

Then she encountered Parry's face, turned toward her with an appealing little-boy-lost expression, and at once she looked back at Luke with a deprecating laugh. "Forgive me for being rude. Of course I'd like to see the grounds again."

"Later, when you're not tired," Luke said, smiling. "Dinner will wait for you."

So that was how the land lay, he thought as he watched them go upstairs together. She was the bait Parry was dangling before him. She could hardly bear to be near him, but she'd do whatever that pretty boy wanted. Contempt for both of them curdled in his stomach.

But then he saw Eve halt briefly in the curve of the stair and look around her, unaware of being watched. And he thought he'd never seen a human face so bitterly unhappy.

Eve and Parry were the last in to dinner and heads turned as they entered, both of them tall, fair and beautiful.

Luke saw that Eve had altered in the space of an hour. She'd looked tired and almost defeated when she'd arrived, but now she'd recovered her courage and walked proudly with a touch of arrogance. She wore a low-cut dress of shimmering black that clung to her slender figure, accentuating the tiny waist and the flair of her hips. Her whole form seemed made to celebrate the joys of physical pleasure, but the remote look on her face hinted at a different story, and the contrast gave her a mystery that went beyond mere looks.

To the casual glance she possessed supreme assurance. Only eyes sharpened by love and hate would notice the tell-tale touch of defiance, as if she were walking on hot coals.

Luke knew his guests were curious. Although he'd always guarded his private affairs fiercely, one or two of them suspected that he'd once been connected with Drummond Lea. His relationship with Eve was still a secret, but he could sense them watching him as he welcomed her back to her old home. Some of them privately called him a barbarian, a man without civilization who achieved his aims by brute force. It was even rumored that his scar was the legacy of a fight with a man he'd ruined. Luke had laughed at that and done nothing to deny the story. Now, as he offered her his arm and led her to her place, he guessed that they were thinking, "Beauty and the Beast."

As Eve took his arm, she came briefly out of her faraway world and smiled, not at him, but again just over his shoulder. It was a proud, gallant smile, and it belied the slight tremor in her fingers that told how much of an ordeal this was for her.

He'd resisted the temptation to seat her beside himself at dinner. Instead he placed her at the foot of the long dining table with Parry on one side of her and another man on the other. From his seat at the head he hoped to see her face, but she was too far away for him to make out much.

He was displeased to find the seat on his right occupied by Lady Vivienne Lloyd, a young woman with whom he'd enjoyed a pleasant liaison and who had subsequently married Denzil Lloyd, one of his friendly rivals. Her father was an earl, but penniless, a deficiency that she'd repaired with the help of a voluptuous frame and a one-track mind. Luke hadn't planned to have her near him, but she confided that she'd switched the place tags.

"I thought we could have a good gossip, darling," she cooed. "I haven't seen you since my wedding. I was so disappointed that you didn't come."

"I nursed my broken heart at home," he said with mechanical gallantry. Eve was talking to the man on her right.

"Whose fault was it that your heart was broken?" Vivienne asked significantly. "It needn't have been that way."

"I yielded to the better man," he said diplomatically. "But I hope you received my wedding gift." His eyes narrowed as Eve turned to Parry and laid her hand gently on his arm.

"It was beautiful," Vivienne assured him. "It made me think what might have been."

When he didn't answer, her sharp eyes followed his gaze down the table and she gave a little laugh. "Not a hope, my darling. She's out of your class."

He swallowed his annoyance at having revealed his thoughts and observed wryly, "Some people would have said that *you* were."

"Oh, *me*, under this useless title I'm dead vulgar," she said with the frankness that was her most engaging trait. "I actually prefer men to be a bit primitive." Her eyes flickered over him suggestively. "But Eve is another matter. I may be a ladyship, but she's a lady."

"Thank you for the advice, but I can assure you I don't have her in my sights." Then it occurred to him that Vivienne knew all the gossip that was going around and he added casually, "I imagine she's practically engaged to her cousin."

"The gorgeous Parry? He's really something, isn't he?"

"I'm surprised he appeals to you. Not primitive enough, surely?"

She chuckled. "Don't be fooled by that pretty face. He's not a caveman like you, but he's highly, shall we say, original? If dear Eve is sleeping with him, she's certainly lead-ing a full life. Be careful, darling! You've spilt your drink.''

He cursed and poured a double whisky, despising him-self for needing it. He steered Vivienne firmly onto another subject, and the dreadful meal proceeded to its finish. By the last coffee Eve hadn't glanced in Luke's direction once.

As the guests rose from the table, Luke walked up to where Parry stood with Eve and said genially, ''Drum-mond, I don't believe you've met Marcus Laine?'' He in-dicated a small man whose nondescript appearance belied his enormous financial power. Parry's eyes opened a little wider at encountering one of the most notable merchant bankers in London, and he shook Marcus Laine's hand al-most reverently.

''Drummond is in the stockbroking line,'' Luke ex-plained to the banker, who murmured something polite. ''I see you've prospered,'' he remarked to Parry, adding with a chuckle, ''At least I never knew a broker who didn't prosper. Everything going well, I take it.''

''Everything is going splendidly,'' Parry confirmed, his eyes on Laine.

''Of course these are difficult times for all of us in fi-nance,'' Luke mused, apparently oblivious to Parry's dis-comfort, ''what with the markets being so volatile recently. Not everyone can cope.''

''A good broker is ready for anything,'' Parry said firmly.

''Naturally. And I dare say you're weathering the storms better than most.''

''I flatter myself my clients will have nothing to com-plain of,'' Parry observed stiffly.

''I'm sure they won't. I'm glad to hear you're doing so well. I was quite worried about you for a while, but now I see I needn't be.'' He clapped Parry on the shoulder and said genially, "Well, now that we've got business out of the way you can just enjoy yourself for the rest of the weekend."

He turned away, pretending not to see Parry's start of dismay. He knew he had to get out of Eve's orbit quickly before his mood grew dangerous. He forced himself to smile at the other guests and invited them for a tour of the house. The older ones accepted, and he endured a dull hour showing them all over the place while his mind was running obsessively on Eve, who'd stayed downstairs with Parry.

When at last they all came down, he found music playing from the radio and an impromptu dance in progress. Eve was partnering Denzil Lloyd and smiling through her boredom as he explained the ramifications of his latest deal. Luke gritted his teeth at how close Denzil was holding her.

When the dance was over everyone voted for another. Luke immediately invited the wife of an elderly colleague and tried to give her his full attention, but it was hard not to look sideways, trying to get glimpses of Eve, who was dancing with a nondescript-looking man. She seemed absorbed in him, and not by so much as a glance did she betray an awareness of Luke.

He felt his temper beginning to rise. She needed his goodwill and she knew it. Yet far from putting herself out to charm him, she was treating him with lofty indifference, as though she were still the daughter of the house and he the boy from the wrong side of the tracks. If she was waiting for him to approach her begging for the privilege of a dance, she'd learn her mistake.

The music stopped and he raised his voice and said cheerfully, "Let's have the ladies choose partners for the next one and find out who's in favor."

There was general laughter. Luke's eyes were fixed on Eve, waiting for her to come to him.

The next moment she'd taken Parry's hand.

The shock of rejection held him rigid, unable to tear his eyes from her as she glided like liquid in Parry's arms, the shimmering dress outlining her movements. Hardly knowing what he did, he lifted his left hand and touched the scar.

And just then she looked up and saw him. For the first time that evening she looked directly at his face, and her glance was filled with understanding and pain. Luke drew in his breath sharply, then turned away.

Four

Late that night when everything was silent Luke stood at his window, watching the L-bend of the house. He could see Parry's window, its curtains drawn, and just enough light coming from behind them to reveal that there were two people inside. He watched those shadows, trying to shut out the memory of Vivienne saying, "If dear Eve is sleeping with him, she's certainly leading a full life." He poured another whisky to dull his raw nerves, then closed his eyes, wondering why he'd inflicted this misery on himself.

He turned away from the window, but it drew him back. At last he fled temptation, leaving the room and going downstairs to slip out on the far side of the house. As he wandered through the grounds, he decided that Eve had been right. He should turn this place into a hotel and never come here again.

He wasn't sure how it happened, but his feet had taken him to the spot beneath her bedroom window. Perhaps it

was an impulse of nostalgia, or perhaps it was the longing
to know if any light came from behind her window. As he
turned the corner he could see the stone terrace where he'd
stood, aching with love for her, until she had come down
and thrown herself into his arms, but he halted, annoyed to
find that he was not alone. A figure was sitting in the shadows, so motionless that it might almost have been a statue.
Then, as he began to back quietly away, she turned, and he
knew who it was.

He tried to tell himself that the feeling that shook him was
hate, but he knew it was joy at discovering that she was not
with Parry and that she, too, had remembered. The sensation was so violent that it left him shaking.

He stood silently watching her as she sat motionless in the
soft starlight, her unseeing gaze on some distant horizon.
Now that she believed herself alone her defiant courage
seemed to have drained away, and the strain of the evening
was clearly marked on her lovely face.

Then she looked up and saw him, and for a moment they
stared at each other, neither speaking nor moving. Luke
could hear his own heart beating, and he had to steady
himself before he could speak calmly. "Shouldn't you have
put on something warm?" he asked, for she'd come out in
her evening dress with nothing to protect her shoulders from
the night air.

"I came out because I was too warm," she said. "I was
suffocating in there."

He didn't have to ask what she meant. He sat beside her
on the low stone terrace. He could see her bare shoulders
gleaming, and her warm, mysterious perfume reached him.
She gave a little shrug, as if resuming a burden she'd briefly
laid down, and when she spoke she'd regained her assurance. "I should congratulate you on how far you've come,

Mr. Harmon," she said, sounding slightly amused. "I'm very impressed."

"If you want to make small talk, I can't do it," he said bluntly. "It's one of the refinements I could never see the point of."

"I dare say there are a lot of those," she observed wryly.

"I make my point in my own way."

"Yes, you were always a direct person. I remember." When he didn't respond to this, she added, "But you've learned *some* subtlety. The way you played with Parry tonight was very cruel."

Luke shrugged. "I merely asked him how he was doing."

"In front of a man like Marcus Laine? What was he supposed to say? That he's in debt?"

"Is he?" Luke asked a little too quickly.

"I didn't say that," she retorted. "But if he was in need of money, he couldn't have said so there and then, as you well knew." Her voice took on a persuasive note. "But you were only teasing, weren't you? You'll talk to him properly?"

"You're wasting your time pleading for him," Luke growled. "It would be better to plead for yourself."

"I'll never plead for myself," she said proudly. "You wouldn't listen." Her voice softened. "And the man I once knew wouldn't have wanted me to plead with him."

"The man you once knew was a fool."

"Perhaps he was," she agreed in a soft voice that made him tremble. "But he was a wonderful fool. He was kind and gentle, and he could never have deliberately hurt anyone."

He was swamped by fury at the cynical ease with which she invoked those memories. Did she think him such a dolt that she could make use of him a second time? "Stop it!" he said harshly. "You're talking about a man you never really knew. Neither of us knew the other. I thought you were the most perfect human being on earth. You thought I was Johnny Raw who could be trodden underfoot without protest. We were both mistaken.''

There was a pause before she said in a constricted voice, ''I never thought that of you. And I never wanted you to think me perfect. Luke, don't judge me without knowing what happened. I did wrong, but not in the way you think. I was stupid, but I loved you.''

His face was livid in the starlight. ''You play your role very well, Miss Drummond. Parry would be proud of you.''

He heard the silence and then the soft intake of her breath. ''If you really believe that, there's nothing I can say. I'd hoped to make you understand and perhaps forgive me. I should have known better, but I hadn't realized how very much you hate me.''

''Don't I have reason to hate you?'' he asked in a low voice.

She gave a cool laugh. ''I'm not sure that you do. You told me only power matters, and I set you on the road to that power, didn't I? Where would you have been without the money you sold me for?''

''Do you think I care about the damned money?'' he demanded violently. ''Haven't you the wit to know that I took it because you'd destroyed everything else for me?''

''Did you? Or was it what you always wanted? Wasn't it all for money, Luke? Didn't I do just what you wanted when I came running after you, so wildly in love that I forgot everything else?''

''But you remembered in time,'' he said with quiet bitterness. ''At the last moment you saw the mud on my boots and realized what life with me would mean. All *I* saw was that you were my goddess. You could have had my life, but it wasn't any use to you, so I took it back and made what I could of it."

"And what you've made of it is cold, hard and destructive. You're going to destroy *me*, aren't you, Luke? Will that make you happy? Will everything be all right then?"

"Nothing will ever be right," he said somberly.

"You didn't have to bring me back to Drummond Lea to tell me that," she said wildly. "I should never have come. There are too many memories."

"Then perhaps it's time we confronted them."

"Why? So that you can teach me to hate as you do? What we had was beautiful. I want to keep it that way. I'm going away tomorrow before you do us any more harm."

She rose and at once he, too, got to his feet to prevent her. But he stumbled over a small table on his left that he hadn't seen and flung out his left hand, groping wildly for safety. He had a dreadful sensation of floundering in a dark fog, then he grasped something and realized that he was holding her. "It's all right," he said curtly. "Let me go."

But she held on to him, looking up anxiously into his face. "What happened?" she asked.

"Nothing. I tell you I'm all right," he snapped.

Her gaze was fixed on his left eye. "You should have seen that table," she said, speaking as though in a daze.

"Nonsense. It's dark out here." He was breathing hard with a kind of dread as her fingers moved up to his scarred eye.

"There's light enough," she said slowly. "Oh, dear God—you couldn't see it, could you? You're blind in that eye."

"Not completely," he said, ceasing to fight her and speaking tiredly, like a defeated man. "By day I have some sight in it. But at night..."

Eve didn't hear him. Tears were pouring down her face as with gentle hands she drew his head down to her, caressing the scar with her fingertips. "I didn't know," she whispered. "I thought—*oh, my love.*"

She pulled him closer to lay her lips over the scar, and he felt her hot tears against his face. For a moment the world seemed to stop. Then he sank back onto the seat and buried his face against her while her arms enfolded him protectively.

One half of him warred with the other. Why was he doing this when he hated her, distrusted her? But reason was useless against the old familiar joy that flooded him at her gentle touch, at the sound of her sweet voice murmuring, "My love . . . my love." He put his arms around her, let her enfold him against herself and knew that he had found his only place of rest.

After a while he felt her hands urging him to raise his head. He did so and at once she laid her lips against his. The kiss destroyed the bitterness of years, breaking down the barriers that had stood so strong against her, as though they were feathers. He'd deluded himself. This woman had only to open her arms to him and he was lost.

"You should have told me," she whispered, kissing the scar. "Who *dared* to hurt you?"

He couldn't answer her directly. Instead he spoke the only word that would come to him, her name, over and over, as though it was a charm to break the evil spell that had turned his heart to ice. He felt himself being reborn under the beautiful tenderness of her lips and hands. Like all births, it was painful, but he didn't fight the pain. It was his salvation.

He found his voice at last. "Why did you leave me?" he asked hoarsely. "How could you do it?"

"I had no choice," she said. "I didn't want to leave you. It broke my heart. I never stopped loving you...."

"Then *why*?"

"Because—" a shudder possessed her "—because I lied to you. It seemed so harmless at the time. I didn't realize I was doing something that could destroy you."

"Lied? About what?"

"About my age. I wasn't sixteen as I told you. I was fifteen. I was so much in love with you, and I was afraid if you knew the truth you'd think me too young, but I was only fifteen when we made love. That's why I kept putting off our elopement. I was waiting to be sixteen. In fact, when I agreed to go with you I was still three weeks away from my birthday. But I knew we had to live in Scotland for three weeks before we could marry there anyway, and I planned to tell you the truth when we'd started the journey.

"But Tyler discovered me as I was creeping out of the house with my suitcase. He made me jilt you and write that note, saying we'd made a mistake. He said if I didn't do just as he ordered, he'd tell the police and you'd be jailed for statutory rape. I pleaded with him to be allowed to see you and explain, but he wouldn't listen. He wouldn't even let me write to you in my own way. I had to word the note just as he said. That's why it was so cold and curt."

"Dear God," Luke whispered.

"What could I do? I was so scared of some harm coming to you, and it half killed me to think it was my fault. I even went abroad the same night because of what Tyler said would happen to you if I didn't. It broke my heart when I got my letters back with what you'd written on them, because I knew I'd always love you."

"Then why didn't you come to find me when you came home?" he demanded.

"Because..." She looked away. "Because of something else Tyler told me."

"What is it?" Luke took her shoulders and drew her back to him. "Eve, don't let there be any secrets between us now. We've found each other and we can be together again."

"But we can't," she cried in agony. "That's the worst of it. We can never be together." She buried her face in her hands.

"I don't understand," he said somberly. "What can keep us apart now?"

"Tyler told me something else—something terrible. I nearly went crazy when I heard about it."

"Then tell me."

"Luke, what did Megan tell you about your parents?"

"My parents?" he echoed, bewildered. "Only that my mother went away and married someone Megan didn't know and that he died before I was born."

"That isn't true," Eve whispered. "Your mother was never married to your father."

Luke was quiet a moment. "I wondered about that sometimes," he said eventually. "Megan was always so hesitant of talking about him. But how does this connect with what Tyler told you?"

He knew, though. And when she asked, "Haven't you guessed who your father was?" he realized that the signs had been there for a long time.

"Tyler," he breathed.

Eve nodded. "He told me that night. It was horrible. He said the time had come to tell the truth, and I must forget about you, because you're really my uncle—"

"But I'm *not*," Luke broke in violently.

"Luke, he told me all about it. He said he'd had an affair with Helen years ago, and when she became pregnant he sent her away."

"Damn him!"

"And then she died when you were born. That's why Megan hated him so much. She brought you back to Drummond Lea to torment him. Didn't she ever tell you all this?"

"She tried, just before she died, but she'd had a stroke and couldn't talk properly."

"I think in his way Tyler hated you, too," Eve said. "That's why he couldn't bring himself to acknowledge you. If he had, if we'd only known the truth in time..."

"We'd have missed loving each other," Luke said fiercely.

"Yes, you're right. I'm glad we had that, even if it was for just a little while."

"We'll have it forever," he said exultantly. "Damn Tyler and his scheming. He just wanted to keep you to himself. So he thought it was time for some truth telling, did he? But he left out the important part because that wouldn't have suited him at all. I'm not your uncle, Eve. There's no blood relation between us."

"But—"

"*I* may be a Drummond, but *you're* not. Your father was a man called Dermott Wilshaw."

He'd half expected her to deny the possibility, but instead she frowned and said, "You mean...my mother's groom?"

"You knew him?"

"He'd worked for her family. She took him with her when she married Dad. They used to go riding together. It...it could be true. I know Dad didn't like him."

"Perhaps he came to suspect. Megan told me he fathered you before she married, *and Tyler knew.* He admitted as much to me over Megan's grave."

She stared at him incredulously, hardly daring to hope. "Tyler told you it was true?"

"He knew there was no blood tie between us. He'd known it for years. He destroyed our love with a deliberate lie."

"Oh, God," she whispered, "all those years wasted. I was like a burden crushing me, knowing that even if we met again it was impossible."

"But we *have* met again and everything is possible," he said in a voice of heartfelt gladness, opening his arms to her.

She went into them with a cry of joy, and in a moment her head was cradled in its old position against his shoulder and her mouth was soft and welcoming against his. He kissed her with fierce delight as though he could recover their lost years all in a moment. "Eve...Eve..." he murmured hoarsely. "Tell me you're still mine."

"Always," she said passionately. "Always yours in my heart."

The old passion flamed in him, stronger and more demanding for the years apart. What they'd once shared hadn't, after all, been a cruel delusion, but the beginning of a true love that had never really died. Beneath the scarred man and the cautious woman the boy and girl still lived and loved each other.

"Do you remember that night when I came here to stand beneath your window?" he whispered, "and you came down to me?"

"Yes." Her answer was almost inaudible, but his heart heard it. "I came because I loved you."

"Love me now," he pleaded.

She grew still, looking up into his face, then a great peace seemed to descend on her, and she took his hand to lead him inside the house. At that moment he would have followed her anywhere. He knew now how Adam had felt in the garden of Eden when Eve had tempted him and he'd followed her, knowing he had no choice, however high the price.

They climbed the stairs together, his hand still clasped in hers, until they reached the half-landing. There he pulled her into his arms again, kissing her long and deeply before lifting her and carrying her the rest of the way to her room. His blood was pounding in his veins as he thought of what was to come, and he was sure she must feel his arms trembling as he held her.

In his room she stopped him from putting on the light. "We don't need that," she murmured.

Half dreaming he began to pull off his clothes. Every inch of him was burning, longing to be naked with her and to feel her against him. In the soft light from the window he watched, entranced, as her dress whispered to the floor and was followed by her flimsy underclothes. At the sight of her body, bathed in silver by the moon, he stood still, feeling that his heart might fail him at so much beauty.

Their youthful lovemaking had been hurried, feverish. There had never been time for him to watch like this and drink in her perfection, noticing the proud peaks of the full, rounded breasts, the tiny waist and flared hips, the long, elegant thighs. He sank slowly onto the bed, gazing at her with hungry eyes, and when she was finished undressing he opened his arms and she came into them. He pulled her tightly against him so that his face came to rest between her breasts. He felt the soft touch of her hands on his hair, the slight pressure as she rested her cheek there, and heard the murmured words of endearment.

Her warmth and femininity enveloped him, wiping out pain and bitterness, taking him to a timeless place where there was only her. The love and desire he'd thought long dead had only slept. Now his beloved's kiss had reawakened them, and they were as bright and vivid as when they'd been newborn in the morning of the world.

He began to move his hands gently over her, reveling in the silkiness of her skin. His fingers explored her back, her tiny waist, the full swell of her buttocks, and he could feel her body warm beneath his touch, welcoming him. He moved his face against her breast, seeking the nipple, finding it, tasting its sweetness. He flicked it with the tip of his tongue, teasing it to a hard peak, driven by a primitive force, older than time, that told him this woman belonged to him. He had almost lost her, but now he was reasserting his possession of her once and for all.

She felt so slim and fragile against his great frame. And so he touched her with gentle reverence, afraid to harm her or break the spell they were creating between them. He only half believed what was happening. It was too much like the visions that had tormented his dreams and that he'd determinedly denied when awake. He'd told himself he could never feel anything but enmity for her, but his heart had known better and had invoked her again and again in his defenseless sleep. Now she was here at last and he was full of fear lest he awake and find himself alone again. He knew he couldn't endure it.

He traced erotic patterns on her breast with his tongue and felt her arch against him and throw back her head in an ecstasy of abandonment. Delight shivered through him at the moan of desire that broke from her. Slowly he leaned backward, drawing her with him until they lay together on the bed, their limbs entwined. He was burning with fever at the feel of her against him. She caressed him, traced his heavy torso and flat stomach. And when she touched his manhood, it was a sweet agony that sent shudders of unbearable pleasure through him.

His control was slipping away, but he forced himself to be patient, and it was only when she whispered, ''Love me, Luke,'' that he parted her legs, seeking her. And to his joy he discovered that the old love was still there, as though it were only yesterday that they'd lain like this, innocent and passionately young, exchanging promises of forever because the world was theirs and nothing could hurt them. And it was true, after all, because as he entered her and felt her welcome him, enfolding him deep in her wonderful tenderness, the hurts fell away as if they had never been and the world was theirs once more.

It was so good to be a part of her again, feeling her responding, arching up to meet him eagerly, wrapping her legs around him. She sent him half mad with pleasure and also something that was more than pleasure, something for which he knew he could never find words. He was pervaded by her perfume of musky warmth and feminine desire, and the intoxicating aroma drove him on, seeking to become more fully one with her.

"Luke," she whispered, *"Luke..."*

He knew that special note in her voice, the note that told him he could abandon all restraint. His coherent mind seemed to disintegrate as pure sensation claimed him, convulsing his body in the rhythm of uncontrollable desire until the moment when the whole world exploded.

He returned to himself with a reluctance so great that it was almost despair. He'd known happiness again and wanted it to last forever. The waning of his body's vigor and the ending of their union seemed to him almost a betrayal, and he was suddenly filled with fear, as though it foreshadowed another parting. He clasped her to him as though it were in his power to defy nature and prolong their loving. And Eve seemed to understand, for she wrapped her arms tenderly about him, murmuring soft words of love that eased his pain, for they held a sweet promise for the future.

Five

———

He awoke in the early morning to find himself still in Eve's arms and lay blissfully content, without moving, listening to the soft, steady beat of her heart. He knew she was awake because he could feel her fingers gently touching his hair. "Wasn't there a legend once," he murmured, "that long ago each man and woman formed one half of a perfect whole? But something divided them, and each half spent its life seeking the other?"

"It sounds likely," she whispered.

"I feel like that. All the time we were apart I was incomplete, and now I know why."

"It was the same with me, but I couldn't admit that I was still in love with you because I thought you were my uncle. When we met again the other day and you kissed me I was appalled at myself because I wanted you as much as ever. I ran away from you, but I couldn't run away from my own feelings. When I thought of spending all my life loving you but cut off from you, I thought I'd go mad."

"Was that why you had that dreadful look on your face when you left me that day?" he asked. "And why you tried to avoid me here?"

"Yes. I was sure I must be a monster to feel as I did about you."

He touched the scar. "I thought it was this, and you couldn't bear to look at me or be near me."

"No," she said fiercely, pulling him closer. "That could only make me love you more. To think that you were hurt, and I wasn't there to comfort you. How did it happen?"

"I'll tell you another time," he said quickly. "Right now I just want to look at you. It's as though I've come alive once more. I've been such a fool. I should have trusted you."

"How could you imagine anything like the truth?" she defended him. "It was my fault for lying to you in the first place, but I was so wild about you. And I suppose I was spoilt. I was used to having what I wanted, and I wanted *you*."

He kissed her nose. "That's very flattering."

"But I didn't look beyond my own wishes. I lied about my age because it was the quickest method of getting my own way. I never thought what I might be doing to you. I was an awful spoilt brat." She laughed suddenly as an echo came into her head, and then fell silent.

"What is it?" Luke asked quickly.

"Nothing... it's nothing."

But he'd seen the shadow on her face and he wouldn't be put off. "Tell me," he demanded imperiously. Then he colored as he saw Eve eyeing him quizzically, and said hastily, "Please, Eve, tell me what's troubling you."

"It's that talking about being a brat reminded me of something Parry said."

Luke's face darkened. "What about Parry?"

"He said *he* was a brat at fifteen, and he told me something that happened between you—about a sack of potatoes."

Luke gave a grunt. "Oh, that."

Eve's face was troubled. "Did you really thrash him with his own riding whip?"

"I walloped his behind. Don't feel sorry for him, Eve. He was asking for it."

"Because he accidentally knocked over your potatoes?" she demanded, scandalized.

"It was no accident."

"He says it was."

"Meaning I'm a liar?" he asked sharply.

"No, of course not. But you could be wrong. You must have been hot and tired, and I expect you overreacted."

"I wasn't wrong," Luke said. "He was pushing his luck and he pushed it too far. He thought because he was a Drummond he could do as he liked and escape the consequences." A new, hard note came into his voice. "But there's always a penalty...in the end."

Eve stared at him. "And you always make people pay it, don't you?"

"Yes," he said simply. "It's the first rule of business...and of life, if a man has any sense. Never let yourself be permanently worsted. Always put the score straight, however long it takes." Then he saw her expression and said quickly, "Not *you*, my darling."

"You were going to make me pay. I know that."

"Eve, please forget all that nonsense I talked," he said quickly. "I was hurt and I wanted to hurt you. I'm not proud of it, but I know now that I was wrong and stupid.

Can't we leave it there and let things be right between us? We love each other, don't we?"

"I'll always love you," she said gravely, "but I'm coming to realize that you're a very frightening man. You judge people in terribly stark terms. You make no allowances for the little pressures that force them to do things they shouldn't."

She tried to silence the memory of Parry saying, *"There was always a touch of the brute about him,"* but it was hard when Luke himself seemed ready to confirm it. She saw now that she'd never really known him, that part of his heart was dark and hidden from her and perhaps always would be. But she also knew that she had no choice but to love him, whatever he was like.

"Let's not talk about this," Luke said quietly. "It comes between us, and I can't bear anything to do that."

She made one last try. "Then perhaps we *should* talk about it and understand each other."

"No," he said firmly. "At least . . . not yet. We have a lot of catching up to do. Let's take it slowly." He spoke in a gentler tone. "Tell me what's happened to you since I last saw you."

"You already know. You were keeping tabs on me, weren't you?"

He gave a half smile, as if in mockery of himself. "I kept any newspaper cuttings like a lovesick fan. I couldn't help it. I told myself it was hate, but I think now I must always have known this would happen. I nearly went mad when I heard about your marriage. Tell me about David Fletcher. Did you love him?"

"No. After you, I was finished with love, so my life had to be built around something else. Art and antiques were the only other things I cared about. I took courses at school in Switzerland, and when I came home I started studying seriously. David was my tutor, and I suppose I saw him through rose-colored spectacles. I was eighteen and full of unrealistic ideas. Only art mattered, and the man who seemed to know all about it looked almost godlike. When he asked me to marry him I was terribly flattered.

"But when we were married the 'god' dwindled into a petty little man, full of vanity, who couldn't bear to have anyone disagree with him. I think he married me because I was an adoring pupil and he thought I'd stay that way. When I started to have opinions of my own, he didn't like it.

"He was immensely knowledgeable in his own line, which was watercolors, but he had odd blind spots, which he wouldn't recognize. Tyler gave me my Drummond shares as a wedding gift, and although David liked having a lot of money he hated the fact that it was mine. He was always trying to pull off a spectacular coup to make a big fortune of his own. In the end he bought a picture, which he convinced himself was an undiscovered Titian, but several Titian specialists refused to authenticate it. It shattered him so much he had a heart attack.

"I'd been about to leave him, but I just couldn't do it then. I stayed and looked after him for the last year. To the end of his life he maintained he'd been the victim of a conspiracy. 'You'll be a rich woman when the truth is known,' he kept saying. He had to believe that because he'd mortgaged everything we had to buy that painting."

"Is there any chance that he was right?"

"No. After his death I had someone run chemical tests on the paint. There are pigments there that weren't invented in Titian's day. David would never allow those tests to be made. I suppose he was afraid to. I sold the picture for about a tenth of what he paid for it. It went to pay off the debts.

"Since then I've tried to make my own career. I became Eve Drummond again because to be David Fletcher's widow wasn't the greatest recommendation in the art world." She sighed. "Poor David. I made him as unhappy as he made me."

"You mean, because of the others?" Luke asked.

"Others?"

He tried to speak lightly. "At our first meeting you implied that there had been more men in your life than just a husband."

Eve touched his face gently. "Has that been worrying you?"

He shrugged. "You were his wife, not mine. I have no right to care about your other men. It's just that . . . I do."

"Well, you needn't. Darling Luke, there were no others. I swear it. Don't take any notice of what I said that time. You were breaking my heart, telling me that all I'd been to you was a way of raising money from Tyler. So I paid you back in your own coin because it was the only way I could preserve my pride. But the truth is that apart from my husband I've never made love with any man but you."

His relief showed so plainly on his face that she kissed him again and again, wondering how such happiness could have come to her, and how long she could dare to hope for it to last.

"Since my relationship with David went sour," she resumed, "I've felt I never wanted to get involved with a man again." She gave a wry laugh. "I'm more at ease with paintings and antiques. It's a pity you can't run chemical tests on a man to see if he's a phony."

"I thought your grandfather was set on you and Parry making a match of it," Luke said, apparently casual but inwardly holding his breath for the answer.

But Eve shrugged and said, "Oh, Tyler changed his mind."

"Why did he do that?"

"I don't know. He never said." She didn't offer to elaborate, not wanting to spoil the atmosphere again. Luke watched her in the semidarkness for a moment, wondering if she'd talk about what Parry had been to her since her husband died. When she didn't he tried to push the moment aside and ignore the slight shadow that lay on his heart.

"What happened that night?" she asked him. "Did you go to meet me, or did you get my letter first?"

"I went to the place where we were supposed to meet and it was given to me there," he said cautiously. He wondered how much he should say now. All his instincts warned him that this would be a bad time to speak of what Parry had done to him.

"Who gave it to you?"

"I didn't see his face," Luke said wryly. "It was dark."

"And you went home and wrote 'Bitch' across my letters before sending them back to me," she reflected. "How you must have hated me."

"But I didn't do that. Someone broke into the cottage and stole those letters."

Her eyes widened. "Tyler went that far?"

"Somebody did."

"Tyler came to Switzerland with me, but he must have left orders that my letters were to be retrieved somehow. I wonder who—"

"We'll talk about it later," he said quickly.

"Yes. Tonight I just want to tell you again and again that I love you. Oh, Luke—"

"Why do you call me that?" he asked, frowning.

"You told me to. It's who you are now."

"Not to you. Everything's the same as it was before when I was John Baxter."

She was silent for so long that he stared at her, disconcerted. "No," she said at last. "It isn't the same as it was, and it never can be. Luke, darling, listen to me." She took hold of him as he made a startled movement. "We're different people now. We've each lived a life away from the other and it's shaped us. That country boy whose face I could always read like an open book has changed into a hard, cautious man, maybe even a cruel man, who keeps his secrets from his friends and enemies. And I think you have a lot of enemies. Maybe you've earned them."

"What does it matter as long as I have no secrets from you?" he demanded.

"But you will," she said simply. "Just as I will, because however much we love each other we're two people, not one, and neither of us knows much about the other. We can't turn the clock back. We must go on from where we are. I can only love Luke Harmon by seeing him as he really is and not pretending that he's someone else."

He ran a hand through his hair. Eve's realism irked and confused him, cutting across his romantic dream of a world where nothing had changed. Her assertion that she, once so open to him, had the right to keep her secrets, fell on his heart almost like a threat. Above all he wanted to believe that she was the same person, but she read the thought in his eyes and shook her head. "You think of me as Eve Drummond, but for years I was Eve Fletcher. I was marked by that marriage."

"It doesn't matter," he growled. "It's over now. The only thing that counts is that we're together." He took her into his arms before she could speak again. "As long as you can still love me," he said.

"I'll always love you, Luke."

He drew her against him, kissing her, speaking her name, and as their desire mounted everything else was forgotten.

When she'd fallen asleep again, Luke rose and put on a light robe. In the rediscovery of their love he'd had no time to think of what Eve had told him. He was Tyler's son.

The knowledge stirred deep feelings, not feelings of love but of recognition. Now he knew why he'd instinctively chosen Tyler's room for his own. Their similarities had always been there, haunting the edge of his consciousness, maddening Tyler with a truth he couldn't or wouldn't admit, and causing much of their mutual antagonism. He had no tender thoughts toward the old man, only bitterness for the past. He thought of his one small photograph of Helen, of her gentle face. He thought of Tyler rejecting her when she was carrying the child they'd made together, and he wished his father could be there now to feel his wrath.

He recalled Tyler standing beside Megan's grave saying that Eve, with no Drummond blood in her, was still a Drummond "because I say so," just as his own son could be dismissed as not a Drummond, because Tyler had so decreed it. For a moment the autocratic imperiousness of such a will roused his reluctant admiration. Then the thought came, wouldn't a normal man feel something for the son who was so like him? And a chill passed across his heart at the knowledge that his father had seen him day after day and had never wanted him.

He seated himself at Eve's dressing table and stared into the large mirror. He could see the resemblance now, less of the face than of the spirit. In the past ten years his features had begun to assume the harshness that had marked Tyler's, as bleak and unyielding as rock.

Suddenly he rose and went quickly to draw back the curtain so that the first light of a brilliant dawn could stream into the room. Its rays woke Eve, who stirred and turned toward him, bathed in light. In a moment he was across the room, taking her into his arms and giving passionate, silent thanks that the darkness was past, because she had returned in time to save him.

There was another day to go before the house party broke up. To Luke and Eve the time seemed interminable. They survived by trying to appear unaware of each other. It was this that gave Luke the insight to notice, with amusement, that Parry Drummond and Lady Vivienne were also pointedly ignoring each other, and Vivienne's husband was looking glum. So now he reckoned he knew whose had been the extra shadow on Parry's curtain that night.

After lunch on Sunday the guests began to leave. Eve and Parry were among the first to go, bidding Luke a polite goodbye with formal smiles. Parry was on edge because he hadn't managed to get Luke to himself for a talk, but at last he had to depart, disappointed.

By early evening Luke was alone. He spent an hour trying to read papers and taking nothing in. Subconsciously he was listening for the sound that would tell him he hadn't imagined everything that had happened. At last it came, the scrunch of tires on gravel, the front door opening, his housekeeper exclaiming, and then Eve's voice growing closer. His heart beat painfully as he opened the door of the study, and in another moment she was in his arms.

After a very long silence, he said, "I thought you were never coming."

"It took me ages to get rid of Parry. He kept wanting to talk, asking me questions. Did I think I'd got on well with you? Would you change your mind about the dividend? And so on. I didn't know what to say."

"You should have told him the truth. In fact, you should have sent him back alone and stayed here with me. Why did we have to go through this performance?"

"Because we must be discreet for a while," she declared between kisses.

"The hell with being discreet," he said raggedly. "I want you."

"And I want you, but I couldn't just stay here while all your guests left. The news would be all over London by to-morrow."

"Let it." He was working on her buttons.

"Shouldn't we go upstairs?" she murmured against his lips.

"Definitely."

They returned to her room where he locked the door and they stripped each other's clothes off, laughing like children playing truant. Then he tumbled her into bed and claimed her like a boy discovering love for the first time, with much vigor and no subtlety. She responded in kind, but then, with the first edge of their desire slaked, she practiced witchery on him, seducing him sweetly until he was in a spin, then surrendering into his arms with an eager wholeheartedness that made her again the girl he'd once known.

His mind and senses reeled with conflicting demands. He wanted to possess her totally, and at the same time he wanted her to still exist apart from him, unpossessed, a dream yet to be won, perhaps unattainable. This contradiction troubled him because, despite his shrewdness in business, in his emotions he was a simple, uncomplicated man, more at home with black and white than shades of gray.

Once she dozed off in his arms and awoke to find him gazing down at her. "What are you doing?" she whispered with a sleepy smile.

"Loving you," he answered. "Adoring you, worshiping you, thinking that no man was ever so blessed, no woman so wonderful."

To his surprise the extravagance of his tribute seemed to worry her. "Don't worship me, Luke," she said. "Just love me."

"It's the same thing."

"But it isn't," she insisted.

"Darling, let me worship you if I want to," he pleaded. "You're every perfect woman that ever existed."

"It's only a little while ago that I was a villainess," she reminded him.

"I was wrong." He brushed aside the memory impatiently.

"Yes, and you're wrong now. Don't put me on a pedestal. I'm not an idol. I'm an ordinary woman. If you insist on seeing me through rose-colored spectacles, it'll be harder when you realize how human and fallible I am. Then you'll turn against me, and I'll be the one to pay."

But he wouldn't listen. Something deep and mysterious in his nature needed to worship the woman he loved. For years that need had been thwarted, twisting and distorting his character, turning him toward cruelty. Now that was over and he was almost light-headed with the relief of yielding to his true instincts. "Darling, you're seeing shadows where none exist," he said, and when she tried to protest he kissed her into silence.

To the astonishment and alarm of his employees, he called his office during the morning to say that he was taking a few days off—or maybe more than a few, he didn't know. Mrs. Grace Allardyce, his superefficient personal assistant, was instructed to call him only in case of emergency. "And it had better be a *real* emergency," he added.

"Mr. Harmon, are you...all right?" she asked nervously.

"Never better in my life, thank you."

"It's just that I've never known you like this before."

He laughed and hung up. "They think I'm mad," he told Eve. "But it's a blessed madness. Only truly sane people know how to be mad like this."

"Fancy you having a poetic streak," she teased him.

"I didn't know it myself. But now I feel that all things are possible for me." They'd wandered outside, and he took a long breath of the bright summer air. "I'm free," he said, and slipped an arm about her shoulder, hugging her against him. "The world began today and you and I are the only people in it. What's the matter?" He'd seen a shadow cross her face.

"Darling, I love seeing you so happy, but it scares me, too. You're soaring high and I'm afraid to see you fall and hurt yourself."

"But why should I ever fall? I have you again and that solves all problems. Not another word. I want to take you around the old places where we used to meet."

"I wish Megan was still here to see us," she said as they walked. "But you said she was dead."

"She died a few days after we last saw each other."

Something in his tone made her look at him curiously. "I think you'd better tell me whatever it is that you've been holding back," she said.

They walked for a while under the green summer trees, their arms entwined, until they reached the shaded hollow where they'd once come to be together. "This is where we should have met that night," she reminded him.

"Yes. But I arrived to find a welcome committee. I don't know how many there were, but it felt like four or five kicking and punching me. They did a good job."

In the appalling silence he saw the truth dawn on her face. She reached up to touch his scar but drew back at the last moment as though she felt she had no right. "Did they... was that how...?" She couldn't bear to frame the question.

"That was how my eye was damaged," he finished. "When they'd finished they pushed your letter into my hand. I read it in the hospital. *Eve...*" He broke off to comfort her, for she'd dropped her face into her hands.

"Oh, God," she wept, "I did that to you."

"Of course you didn't. You couldn't have known what was going to happen. Don't cry, my love. It's all over."

"How can it ever be over?" she asked huskily.

He cupped her face in his hands and spoke tenderly. "It was finished as soon as we found each other again. And it'll stay finished as long as we love each other."

She stroked the scar with gentle fingers. "I'll never forgive Tyler for this."

"Eve, it wasn't Tyler. It was Parry."

She stared at him in shock, then shook her head vigorously. "No, that's impossible. Luke, what are you saying? He was a schoolboy."

He laughed cynically. "He was like no other schoolboy. Even then he kept some very dubious company, and Tyler gave him far too much money. He could easily have paid a few violent youngsters to do his dirty work."

"You actually saw Parry there?"

"I didn't see anyone. It was too dark. But I heard that crazy giggle of his. He was enjoying it."

"Luke, you're terribly wrong. You must believe me. Tyler was a harsh man and he was your enemy even though you were his son, or perhaps *because* you were. He could have done this dreadful thing, but Parry? Never. I know Parry. He couldn't hurt a fly."

"That I can believe," Luke said grimly. "But he'd enjoy standing by while others did the hurting for him. I tell you I know it was him. I heard him."

"If you were being attacked by thugs, you can't be sure what you heard," she argued. "You always disliked Parry, although you had no reason to, and you want to blame him for everything, but this is all fantasy."

"Is it?" he said with the beginnings of anger. "It was because I heard Parry's voice that I blamed *you*. You kept putting off our elopement until he came home. That seemed to tie up."

"It was just a coincidence. I've told you I was waiting for my sixteenth birthday. I can understand your making such a mistake then, but surely you can understand now how wrong you were?" When he didn't answer, she looked anxiously into his face and said, "When I think of how cruel and implacable Tyler was that night... Can't you see that it makes more sense for it to be Tyler?"

He turned sharply away from her, distressed at her championing of his tormentor. "Whoever did it killed Megan," he said harshly. "When she came to the hospital and saw my battered face, she collapsed."

"You said once that Tyler was at her funeral," Eve recalled.

"Yes. That was where he offered me five thousand pounds. I refused it at first. Then I went home and found the place ransacked and your letters gone, so I rang him and told him the price was ten. I didn't mean to sell you, Eve. I just didn't care about anything anymore."

"I don't blame you now for taking his money," she said. "But don't you see that it proves it was Tyler who had you beaten up?"

"I think it proves that he didn't," Luke said stubbornly. "He wasn't the man to be sorry for anything he'd decided to do. But if he suspected Parry had gone behind his back, he'd have tried to buy himself a clear conscience."

"You're determined to believe it was Parry, aren't you?" she cried, "Even though it makes no sense. Tyler wouldn't have given my letter to a schoolboy to deliver."

"No, I think he gave it to a servant, and Parry did a little eavesdropping. That would be his style. When Tyler had left for Switzerland with you, Parry bribed the servant to hand it over. He had a score of his own to settle after the way I walloped him, and it would be like him to protect his own skin by working in the dark and letting others do the rough stuff."

She took hold of his arms and stared anxiously into his face. "Luke, you don't *know* any of this. It all springs from your dislike of Parry. Why won't you see that it *must* have been Tyler."

"And why won't you even consider that it might have been Parry?" he growled.

"Because it's impossible." She sighed and pulled his head down until his forehead rested against hers. "It would be dreadful if the two men who are dearest to me in all the world are going to be enemies."

It hurt him to hear her say that Parry was dear to her, but he was so melted with love that he couldn't bear any hint of discord between them. Later, he was sure, he could make her see her cousin more realistically. "Let's drop the subject if it makes us argue," he said gruffly. "We have other things to talk about. Will you want to live here when we're married?"

She didn't answer at once but walked on with a slight frown on her face. He was puzzled but not dismayed, for it was so clear to him that their marriage was inevitable that he hadn't considered that she might disagree. "Luke," she said at last, "let's think about marriage later."

"What do you mean? Of course we must get married."
He hugged her. "We've been engaged for ten years. Don't
you think that's long enough?"

She laughed but said, "I don't think we ought to rush into
it."

"You're serious, aren't you?" he asked incredulously.
"But what is there to wait for?"

"Perhaps we should get to know each other first."

"We've loved each other for ten years. What more do we
need to know? Darling, we've lost a lot of time. Let's not
waste any more."

She smiled tenderly. "Did you know that you're a terrible romantic?"

"Me?" he cried indignantly.

"Yes, you are. You think we can just take up where we
left off. I want to feel that you love me as I am now. Otherwise we have no chance. Can't you see that?"

"All ı can see," he said quietly, "is that if you won't
marry me my life has no meaning. Don't do this, Eve. I've
endured without you for so long. I can't endure any longer.
Nothing can change my love for you. *Nothing*. Do you understand? You're everything to me. I *need* you. I can't
imagine not loving you and needing you." He was suddenly frantic with fear. "I don't know what to say to convince you," he said desperately.

"You've already said it," Eve said, taking his face between her hands. "If you need me, I can't refuse. Oh, my
love...my love..."

Six

They eloped. They ran away to Scotland as they'd meant to once before, slipping out of the house without a word to anyone and hurrying to Luke's waiting car. They made a few concessions to the passing of time. The old banger had been replaced by a Rolls and, instead of driving all the way, they went only to the airport, where they caught the plane for Edinburgh. "I told Mrs. Carter we'd be gone awhile, but I didn't say where," he chuckled as they drank champagne on the flight. "I think she knew, though."

"I like it better this way." Eve sighed happily. "No prying eyes. Why do you keep looking at your watch?"

"I'm calculating how long it will be before I can make love to you."

"That depends on how long it takes us to get married," she said mischievously.

"If you think I'm waiting that long," he growled, slipping an arm around her shoulders.

"We've got to find somewhere to stay first," she reminded him, her head on his shoulder. "Perhaps we should have called ahead to a hotel."

"It's more fun to be spontaneous," he insisted, and his answer silenced her, because she remembered how little there had been in his life that could be called fun.

At the Edinburgh airport he hired a car and drove into town, looking for somewhere to stay. But it was the week before the city's annual Arts Festival, and the hotels were already full. After a lot of driving around and frustration, they found a small guest house in a side street, where the solid middle-aged lady at the desk informed them that there were vacancies.

"I'm Miss Macgregor. I'm the proprietor and manager. Ye'll be letting me know if ye want anything," she said kindly. "Are ye here for the festival?"

"No, we're going to get married," Luke told her without thinking.

The next moment he regretted his frank words because she beamed and said, "Ye'll be wanting two rooms, then."

Luke opened his mouth to dispel this curious idea, saw Eve shaking her head and looking at him with eyes brimming with fun, and closed it again. The arrogant self-confidence born of a thousand victories in boardrooms collided with implacable Scottish respectability and retired defeated. "Thank you," he said meekly.

Eve kept her mirth under control as they went upstairs. Luke glowered but couldn't say anything in front of Miss Macgregor. Eve's room turned out to be comfortable and spotlessly clean, but the bed was uncompromisingly single.

Ten minutes later, while she was unpacking, her bedside telephone rang. It was Luke. "I'm on the next floor up," he said in outrage. "And may I ask what the hell is so funny?" For Eve was crowing with laughter.

"You are," she said when she could speak. "You wanted everything to be as it would have been before, and it is. Oh, heavens!" She went off into another paroxysm while Luke ground his teeth audibly on the other end of the line.

There was no room service, so any idea of a romantic dinner for two was abandoned and they ate downstairs in the tiny dining room. But here things improved, for the food was magnificent, and Luke's mood mellowed under the impact of roast venison, a pungent local cheese and a malt whisky that he declared to be the finest he'd ever tasted.

At last it was time to go to bed. Luke accompanied Eve to her room and defiantly slipped inside with her, although he couldn't resist glancing up and down the corridor first. It annoyed him to find himself acting like a guilty schoolboy, but the atmosphere of the place was beginning to get to him. Inside he took her into his arms and drank deeply of the honey and wine of her lips. "Again," she pleaded. "We don't know how long we may have."

"You don't think I'm leaving now that I'm here, do you?" he growled. He eyed the narrow bed. "It'll be like making love on top of a fence but we'll manage somehow." He claimed her lips again, but a knock on the door stopped him in his tracks.

"I'm just coming in to turn down the bed," Miss Macgregor called.

"There's no need," Eve called back desperately.

"Och, it's nae trouble" came the cheerful response.

Luke groaned. Eve pushed him quickly into the tiny bathroom and opened the door. Miss Macgregor bustled in and busied herself in the already immaculate little bedroom while Eve leaned casually against the bathroom door, ready to fend off any attempt at entry. At last Miss Macgregor finished. "I'll be on my way upstairs now." She raised her voice in the direction of the bathroom. "I'll reach your room in about ten minutes, Mr. Harmon," she called, and departed without waiting for an answer.

"We leave this place tomorrow," Luke declared as he emerged from the bathroom with what little dignity he had left, "unless you want me to have a nervous breakdown."

"Leave it to me." Eve chuckled. "I've got a plan that'll make everything all right."

She gave him a final kiss and sent him off in a daze. He spent a tortured night, aching for her, and finally fell into a light doze, from which he awoke in a state of tension. A call from Eve on the phone cheered him up, only to dash him down again when she told him to go down and start breakfast without her as she was going out. "I'll come with you," he said at once.

"No, I'll see you at breakfast."

"Eve, why are you being so mysterious?"

"You'll find out."

Downstairs he found a young woman at the reception desk and asked for the bill. "We'll be leaving as soon as breakfast is over," he said.

He went and sat at the table with his eyes fixed on the door, through whose windows he could see the main entrance. Miss Macgregor appeared and addressed him with, he thought, misplaced joviality. "Did ye sleep well?"

"Splendidly, thank you," he lied.

"Will I be serving ye now, or will I wait for Miss Drummond?"

"I've no idea when she'll be here," he said morosely.

"In that case I'll serve ye."

The meal was splendid: homemade Scottish porridge with a generous helping of cream, followed by eggs, bacon, sausages and tomatoes cooked by someone who'd mastered the elusive art of producing a decent breakfast. Luke ate as much as he could, but he felt uncomfortable sitting alone with Eve's place conspicuously empty. Miss Macgregor eyed him with deep sympathy and pressed more sausages on him.

Then suddenly he saw Eve coming through the street door, and summer seemed to come with her. Her face wore a small, private smile as though she'd just brought off a trick, and she didn't notice his wave. Luke saw her go to the reception desk and speak to the young woman. They talked earnestly, and he could see that the receptionist was explaining something to Eve, probably that he'd already settled the bill. Eve shook her head vigorously, and to Luke's horror the receptionist began to turn over the pages of the register and pencil something in.

At last Eve came into the breakfast room, saw him and hurried over. "Where have you been?" he demanded.

She smiled. "Making plans."

"I've just paid the bill and told them we're leaving today," he said firmly.

"Really? I've just booked the rooms for the next three weeks," Eve said with a mischievous look.

She thumped him on the back as he choked on his coffee. The paroxysm lasted several minutes because he kept trying to talk through it, but only odd words, like "madwoman" and "in hell first," were audible.

"If you'd let me finish," she said when the worst was over. "We're only going to rent the rooms, not stay in them. As long as we're registered here, we satisfy the residence requirements, and who's to know if we're actually somewhere else?"

"Now you're talking," he said thankfully.

"I've been at the tourist office this morning."

"To find us another hotel?"

"Wait and see." She refused to say more.

After breakfast they fled to the car, leaving token baggage in their rooms. Next came a stop at the town hall where they booked the wedding date. "Now I'm in your hands," Luke said when they were in the car again.

She directed him and he headed the car out of Edinburgh as fast as the law allowed. The city fell away behind them; the scenery began to grow wild. They rolled down the windows and felt the sun and wind on their faces. They passed through villages where time seemed to have stood still and along country roads beside quiet stretches of water. Hills, covered in purple heather, appeared in the distance and, beyond them, mountains that grew more bleak and rugged as they neared. Luke didn't know where they were going, and now that he had Eve to himself he didn't care. All that mattered was to be with her.

At last they arrived at a small village near the shore of a loch. Eve asked some directions and they drove on another mile. "Wait here," she said, and got out of the car in the middle of what might have been the main street. Luke saw her knock at the door of a house and a moment later an old woman answered. He couldn't hear what they said, although he thought he caught the words "Mr. and Mrs. Smith" just before the old woman handed a key to Eve.

"Who are Mr. and Mrs. Smith?" he asked as she got back into the car.

"We are, and for the next three weeks we live at Thistle Cottage, which is just at the bottom of the next street." She laughed at his astonished expression. "I told the man at the tourist board that I wanted to rent a cottage in an out-of-the-way place. He had a list of people who do short summer lets, and all it took was a phone call."

"You're incredible!" he exclaimed in delight.

"Wait until you see it before you say that. He warned me that it's a bit basic."

"I was brought up in a place like that," he reminded her. "You're more likely to be worried about it being basic than I am."

"I won't care," she said, squeezing his hand.

They found the little house without difficulty. It was the last one before the village petered out into moorland. It had flagstone floors covered with rag rugs, heavy, polished oak furniture and a huge window through which the distant glint of water could be seen. "That's Loch Katrine," Eve informed him.

"That's fantastic," he agreed, dropping his head so that he could nibble her ear.

"And just beyond it—"

"Why don't you tell me later?" He was working on her buttons.

"Luke, don't you think we should—"

"No," he said explosively before covering her mouth with his own.

It felt like a million years since they'd last made love, and he was hungry for the feel of her against him. He rained kisses over her face while his hands explored the fastenings of her clothes. The rampant urgency of his desire made subtlety impossible. "Where's the bedroom," he murmured thickly.

"I don't know," she managed to say.

"Then let's find it before I go crazy."

The first door they tried turned out to be the right one, and behind it there was a large, comfortable-looking double bed. They worked feverishly at each other's buttons, throwing their clothes in all directions in their eagerness. It had started as his initiative, but her passion swiftly rose to match his and it was she who pulled him down onto the bed, offering her yearning flesh to his caresses. He came over her almost at once, settling between her parted legs.

It was unbelievably good to have her enclose him deeply, release him halfway then draw him back, anticipating his thrust with a movement that told him how much she wanted him. He let out a long groan in which delight, torment and satisfaction were equally mingled, and she understood at once, arching herself up against him, her head thrown back in erotic abandon.

This was different from other lovemaking when their passion had always been tempered by tenderness. Now they were simply enjoying each other with raw, frantic lust, the kind that only two people who were supremely confident of each other's love could risk. It was powerful, primitive and glorious, and looking down into Eve's flushed face Luke knew that she, too, had been caught up by a primeval force that went back to the dawn of creation.

He could feel her fingers digging into his shoulders as her moment approached. The stream of energy surging through him peaked, driving his loins with ever-increasing speed so that he went hard into her again and again and heard her cry out with ecstasy at the same moment that he seemed to explode.

Afterward they looked at each other gasping, bewildered, knowing they'd crossed into new territory. The next moment they grinned almost sheepishly and clung to each other, laughing. "I'm ravenous," he declared. "Do you think our landlady has stocked the kitchen for us?"

"Luke, I have a confession to make," Eve said, ducking her head in mock humility. "Perhaps I should have told you before. I mean, it's the kind of thing a man likes to know about a woman before he marries her—" she was playing with the edge of the sheet "—and if it makes you change your mind I'll quite understand...."

"Eve, what are you talking about?" he demanded, seriously alarmed.

She looked up at him, her eyes full of mischief. "I'm utterly useless in a kitchen," she admitted. "I can barely boil an egg."

For a moment he, who had enjoyed so little merriment in his life, hovered on the verge of anger that she should frighten him about nothing. Then the impishness in her face got to him and he began to laugh. He told himself that his demons mustn't be allowed to darken her life. He would learn to change and let her lead him into a brighter world. "Luckily I'm a good cook," he said. "Megan made me learn. She said no man should be helpless." He nuzzled her. "Let me cook for you. I'll enjoy it."

They found basic provisions in the kitchen, and he made tea and sandwiches, which they took back to bed and munched in blissful contentment. "This was the best idea you ever had," he said.

"Mmm, I'm pretty brilliant, aren't I?" she agreed.

"Totally." He kissed her.

They cleared the bed of crumbs and settled down again. Almost at once Eve was asleep, one arm holding on to Luke. He was bemused by her ability to drop off at a moment's notice. Her reactions were as straightforward as a healthy young animal's. Despite his solid appearance, it was he who was the restless one, sometimes lying awake into the early hours brooding, whereas she would have put the problem into a separate compartment and shut the door on it until the next day.

By the same token she awoke an hour later, completely refreshed and alert. Luke had spent the time awake, watching over her. She got up onto her knees and threw her arms high, throwing her head back and stretching gloriously. The brilliant afternoon sunlight streamed in through the window, revealing every detail of her silky perfection. Luke drew in his breath at the full, curved breasts, the nipples pointing high as she arched her back. The golden light flooded her, accentuating the firm, rounded buttocks and long, elegant thighs.

Luke clasped his hands around her tiny waist and drew her nearer until he could press his lips between her breasts. She smelled deliciously of sleep and satiety, and he buried his face blissfully against her. "It's been such a long time since we made love," he murmured.

"An age," she agreed, her fingers working in his hair and on the back of his neck in a way that sent tremors through him. "And I want you to make love to me so very much. I want all of you, Luke."

"You just had to mention it," he said, letting his hands drift lower to where he could cup her behind. "All of me is right here at your service. Let me do what you like, my darling."

"Do you know what I like?" she whispered.

"Of course I know. You like to savor love and luxuriate in it...like this." He moved his lips across the surface of one breast until they found the nipple and encompassed it. He drew his tongue very, very slowly against it, and she moaned blissfully, *"Luke..."*

"Mmm," he responded, absorbed in his task. The feel of the hard peak against his tongue was a delight and a provocation, making him wonder how long they could both hold out before desire overcame control. He resolved to make it as long as possible.

Eve dropped her head and her hair swung softly against his shoulder. He could hear her breath come in deep, longing sighs, then her voice, close to his ear, whispering, "Oh, yes, my love...yes...like that..."

He treated the other nipple in the same way and knew by the convulsive movements of her hands in his hair that he was driving her crazy with a need that was a reflection of his own. They were so well attuned that they reacted as one, and the desire streaming through her body was simply a continuation of his own.

He drew her down onto the bed with him and rolled her onto her back. She gave a sigh of satisfaction and tried to pull him over her, but he resisted, smiling. "All in good time," he teased.

"No, now, Luke, please."

"I haven't finished what I'm doing yet," he said, dropping his lips to her waist.

"But I can't wait," she protested, half laughing, half indignant.

He pretended not to hear and went on dropping small kisses on her. Eve gave a shuddering sigh, running her fingers through her hair and arching against him, turning this way and that for him to find new places. The lightest touch of his lips burned her and her skin seemed unbearably sensitive everywhere as though her entire body was holding itself in eager readiness for what was to happen.

He'd turned so that he could kiss the tender skin of her inner thighs. The movement gave her the chance to seek him and close her fingers around his maleness. She held him, feeling the hot, hard power of his desire, wondering where he got the control not to take her now. She started to move her fingers gently, provoking him, and when he looked at her she laughed and said teasingly, "Two can play at that game."

She knew immediately that she'd succeeded. He was over her in a swift, purposeful movement, seeking the place that was eager for him and sliding in with a long, pleasurable sigh that seemed to come from them both at once. And now it was no longer a game. Love and passion mingled inextricably together, spiraling up into infinity, into another dimension. Luke looked down on her face, seeing her eyes shining at him in wonder and feeling her thighs clasped around him in a movement more eloquent of welcome than any words.

The wild joy in his loins grew more demanding. He wanted to take everything and give everything, to love her and to *be* her, just as she had become him in a fusion so perfect that there was no knowing where one ended and the other began. As their moment came they ceased to call each other's name, for their separate identities no longer existed, and their final, mutual surrender was like a confirmation of fate, leaving them drained, happy and full of gratitude.

After breakfast the next morning they went out into the village and paid a visit to their landlady, a smiling, elderly woman called Mrs. Cameron who asked if the cottage was to their liking. Luke detected the hint of anxiety in her voice, and his eyes flickered over her little dwelling, so like the one where Megan had raised him. He guessed that Mrs. Cameron relied on the letting of her cottage to supplement a meager income. "Perhaps it's no what ye were expectin'," she said, eyeing Eve's expensive clothes. "The kitchen..."

Eve had gulped when she saw the kitchen, but now she broke in warmly, "The kitchen is just fine. I'm managing wonderfully well."

"May you be forgiven," Luke murmured into her ear.

Luke paid the first week's rent and they hurried out of the dark little house into the sunshine. Later, when he looked back on their time in Scotland, that one image stayed with him. Eve had taken him out of darkness into light, and there they would always live together.

In the three weeks they spent by Loch Katrine there were several rainy days, but it was the sun he remembered, flooding their lives with its golden warmth as they wandered through the hills and by the water, exploring some of the most ruggedly beautiful scenery he'd ever seen. They enjoyed the rainy days just as much; then they stayed at home exploring each other's heart and mind and body. They fled company and spent every possible moment alone, bathed in their love, reveling in its gifts.

There was only one moment when he felt ill at ease and that was when Eve received a letter from Parry and explained it by saying that she'd dropped him a line. Luke had a sudden jarring sensation, as though a discord had vibrated painfully through him. He hadn't even known she'd written to Parry, and it reminded him that there were parts of her life still secret from him. He pushed the thought aside and didn't ask about the content of Parry's letter. Nor did she offer to read it to him.

"Do you know that's the seventy-second time we've made love since we arrived here?" he said to her one morning as they lay curled up together.

"I know you're a tycoon, but must you bring figures into everything?" she said, chuckling.

"I can't help it. Besides, every single one stands out in my mind."

"Mmm. I'm different. For me it's one big, glorious loving. When I think that only a few weeks ago my life seemed so dreary and futile."

"Do I make you happy, Eve?" he asked on a note of pleading.

"I didn't believe anyone could ever be this happy," she whispered. "I'm afraid. I know it's going to be taken away from us."

"Why should it?"

"Because no one is allowed to be like this for long."

"Nonsense. We've found each other and nothing's ever going to tear us apart again." He took her into his arms before she could answer.

When he awoke later he found her standing at the end of the bed, gazing up at a picture that hung on the wall. It was a small watercolor, executed in dark tints, and it seemed to represent a valley beneath a thunderstorm. Luke had thought it depressing. "That's right," he said as Eve reached up to remove it from the wall. "I've been meaning to take it down. It's hideous."

"And I thought you had an eye for a good business deal," she mocked. "If this is what I think it is, it's worth a lot of money."

"You're making fun of me."

"No, honestly." Eve looked closely at the picture. "I think this was done by Rushmore Selkirk."

Luke stared at her, baffled. "Of whom the world says...?" he enquired at last.

"He was a Scottish watercolor artist who died 150 years ago. He was a boisterous rogue, always drinking and wenching and gambling. He spent half his life on the run from creditors. But he produced marvelous, delicate little pictures that became valuable long after his death. His work is much sought after and very rare. I've been wondering about this picture for days, but I couldn't believe I'd be lucky enough to discover a Selkirk. If this belongs to Mrs. Cameron, she's better off than she thinks."

"Come on, darling, I'd like to do something for the old dear as well, but this is wishful thinking. I know you're the expert, but even I can see that thing's not worth anything."

But Eve insisted on taking the picture along to Mrs. Cameron, who said it had been left to her by her grandfather, who'd had it from *his* grandfather. "Not that he wanted it," she explained, "but the laddie who painted it owed him money and couldn't pay, so he gave Jock Cameron some of his wee pictures instead."

"Some of?" Eve echoed excitedly. "You mean there are more?"

"Aye. I've one or two. Would it be important?"

"It could be very important," Eve confirmed.

After a good deal of rummaging, Mrs. Cameron produced two more pictures tucked away in old paper bags. Eve peered at them closely and was finally able to point out the name Selkirk, very small, in the bottom right-hand corner of each one. It was clear to Luke that the name meant no more to Mrs. Cameron that it did to him. "Och, those old things are nae worth anything," she protested when Eve explained.

But Eve was like a hound that had scented the fox and wouldn't be put off. "If they're real Selkirks, the three pictures might be worth several thousand pounds," she persisted. "Can I use your phone?"

Bemused, Mrs. Cameron agreed, and Eve got straight on to someone in London whom she called Alexander. Luke watched her, fascinated by this new glimpse of her, praying that she wouldn't be too sad when the inevitable disappointment came. Whatever she might tell herself, those pictures belonged in a jumble sale. Mrs. Cameron thought so, too, for she chuckled and offered Luke "a wee dram," which they drank together.

When Eve hung up, she looked pleased with herself and said "wait and see" in answer to his pleas for information. Ten minutes later the phone rang, and Mrs. Cameron answered to find herself talking to a stranger.

"He's coming straight over from Glasgow to look at the pictures," she said in bewilderment when she'd hung up.

Eve nodded. "Alexander said he'd contact his Glasgow agent."

"Do I get to learn who Alexander is?" Luke enquired.

"He's a friend of mine, a London art dealer," Eve explained. "He was thrilled when I told him I'd found some Selkirks, but he said not to get too excited."

Luke patted her hand. "He was right, darling. We all dream of discovering buried treasure, but the odds are against it."

She smiled. "All right, all right, patronize me. I'll have the last laugh."

And she did. The agent arrived an hour later, looked over the pictures and offered twelve thousand pounds for the three. Luke assisted Mrs. Cameron to a chair and poured her another dram. Then he had one himself. Eve was looking different again. She'd brought off a stunning coup and all his business instincts applauded. The fact that he privately thought the pictures hideous only increased his respect for her expertise.

"So that's what you're like when you're in action," Luke observed when they were tucked up in bed that night sharing a bottle of champagne.

"Mmm," she said happily. "I told you I did some freelance scouting. I'm not a real expert. I couldn't have authenticated those Selkirks myself, but I often alert Alexander or other dealers. Mostly it's just small things, but now and then you make an important discovery, like today. That's a real thrill."

"It was very impressive," he agreed. "Twelve thousand pounds out of thin air. I wish I had a few on my staff like you."

She winced. "It's not the money, Luke, although I'm delighted for Mrs. Cameron's sake. It's the joy of finding something of real beauty that nobody dreamed was there.

Hey, what are you doing?" For Luke had removed the glass
from her hand and set it down.

"Reminding you that pictures aren't the only things of
real beauty," he said, taking her into his arms.

Seven

Two days before the wedding they drove back to Edinburgh and returned to Miss Macgregor's guest house, where she assured them, smiling, that everything was just as they'd left it. Luke groaned but allowed himself to be shown, without protest, to his room. When they met again at dinner, Eve had looked over her wardrobe and decided she had nothing suitable to marry in. "Good," he said at once. "We'll enjoy ourselves getting your wedding outfit."

"We?"

"Why not?"

The next day he went to a fashionable shop with her and sat, incongruous but determined, on a small gilt seat while she tried on various outfits. Now and then he offered a comment, but after being firmly quelled by his bride and the sales assistant, he relapsed into happy silence. He was reveling in a pleasure totally new to him. Eve looked glorious in outfit after outfit. She possessed a special quality that brought something extra to clothes. It was more than her astonishing beauty, more even than style. She had the panache of a woman who'd survived bitter experience with a reckless laugh. Luke looked at her with adoration.

"Which do you think?" Eve asked when they'd narrowed the choice down to three.

"We'll take the lot," he announced.

"But, darling," Eve protested, laughing, "I can't wear three."

"Wear one at the wedding and the rest some other time."

"But they're all hideously expensive."

"All the better." He was delighted to buy her more than she could have bought for herself.

He enjoyed himself without stint the rest of the day, loading her down with gifts, giving her everything he'd have liked to give her long ago. Absorbed in his happiness, he failed to notice that Eve's face occasionally wore a shadow for the first time since they'd run away. And when she knew he was looking at her, she quickly banished all signs of care.

If pressed, Eve would have found it hard to say why she was troubled. But she'd seen something on his face that reminded her disturbingly of David when he'd beheld the supposed Titian. David's eyes had held triumph, as though a lifetime's yearning had come to fruition, bringing repayment of all bad debts and compensation for all disappointments. It had been a gloating look, and although she vehemently rejected that word in connection with Luke, she felt that his eyes contained as much possessiveness as love. Her uneasiness grew as she remembered David's other expression, the one he'd worn when his dreams had turned to dust, and she prayed that Luke's face might never look so gray and withered because of her.

This big, assertive man seemed to her so frighteningly vulnerable in his utter certainty that they'd reached safe harbor that she longed for a way to make him understand the dangers. But she knew that words of warning were useless. His happiness had made him deaf to them.

On the night before their wedding they wandered along Princes Street, arms entwined. High above, the great castle rose in floodlit splendor, traffic roared past and people swirled about them, but they saw and heard nothing. They were lost to everything but their profound joy in each other. "Tell me again that you love me," he pleaded.

But she smiled and shook her head. "It would be like telling you that there are stars in the skies. If you don't know by now, you never will."

"You never ask me if I love you."

She shook her head again, this time looking serious. "It can't be told in words. Oh, Luke, shall I tell you what I hope for more than anything in the world?"

"Whatever it is I'll give it to you," he said at once.

"I wonder if you can."

"Tell me."

"It's that we should come to understand each other and judge each other generously."

He stared. "I don't know what you're talking about."

"No, darling," she said softly. "But one day you will. Oh, Luke, my love . . . hold me. Never let me go."

He couldn't sleep that night. Eve's words stayed with him. He was learning that there was more to her than he'd ever dreamed, and perhaps after all it would take time to understand all the facets to her personality. Yes, he decided. That must be what she'd meant. As for "judging each other," he dismissed it as one of Eve's funny ideas.

The following day, in the town hall of Edinburgh, in the presence of the registrar and two professional witnesses, he slipped a ring onto her finger and called her his wife. The

look of disbelieving wonder on her face was enough to
banish the last of his fears.

Afterward they flew to London, arriving at the airport
just past midnight. Luke's chauffeur was there to drive them
home, and they traveled to Drummond Lea sitting in the
back of the car, with Eve asleep on Luke's shoulder. Now
and then he would tighten the arm that held her and drop his
lips to her forehead in a kiss of inexpressible tenderness.
Once he cradled her face in his other hand, drawing it up so
that he could brush his lips against hers. She murmured but
didn't awake, and he let her sink back without disturbing
her further. He was possessed by a deep, all-pervasive happiness such as he'd never thought he'd know again.

The night was almost over when they reached home. Eve
tumbled into bed and went right back to sleep. She was half
awakened a few hours later by Luke brushing her gently
with his lips and murmuring, "I must go to work. I'll see
you tonight. Go back to sleep."

It was the noise of the bedside telephone that awakened
her again. "Evie?" came Parry's voice over the phone.
"Thank heavens you're back. I've got to see you."

"Yes, thank you, Parry, I had a wonderful time," she
said sarcastically.

He made an impatient sound. "Of course I hope you had
a lovely time and all that. But this is really important. Evie,
I *must* meet you today. Can you come up to town?"

"You're a spoilt brat," she said good-humoredly. "All
right, I'll be there in a couple of hours."

"I'll buy you lunch at Pipistrello." He hung up.

She drove the thirty miles to London in her silver sports
car. Pipistrello was one of the city's most luxurious restau-
rants. A beautiful, expensively dressed woman was no rar-
ity, but even so, Eve turned heads when she entered. Parry
rose from a table in the corner to greet her. "Darling, you

look wonderful," he said, kissing her cheek. "Isn't that a new outfit?" Parry never failed to notice what a woman was wearing.

"Yes, I bought it in Edinburgh," she said, sitting down and noting with pleasure that Parry had her favorite aperitif already waiting for her. She sipped it. "Lovely."

"I thought so. It has a certain naive charm."

"You didn't bring me up here to talk about clothes," she said. "What's so urgent, my dear? Come on, tell big sister."

He groaned. "What is it always?"

"Money?" She indicated their surroundings. "You don't eat like a poor man."

"What's one lunch more or less? Besides, this is *the* place to be seen to prove you're a success."

As if to prove it, Marcus Laine smiled at Eve from a distance and gave her a little old-fashioned bow, but his eyes flickered dismissively over Parry, and he didn't try to join them.

"Half the people around you can't actually afford this place," Parry muttered to Eve, "but neither can they afford not to be seen here."

"Parry, what are you covering up?" Eve asked urgently.

"Ruin, darling. Stark ruin, unless I can lay my hands on two hundred thousand pounds."

Eve gasped. *"How much?"*

"You knew I needed money," he said, leaning toward her and speaking softly.

"Yes, but not that much. Parry, what have you been doing?"

"Never mind. You promised to help, but you vanished and forgot all about my problems. Evie, I'm desperate. You've got to help me."

"But I can't raise two hundred thousand. Surely you can see that."

"All I can see is that if I don't get it I'm headed for jail."

Eve stared at him. "What do you mean?"

Parry shrugged. "I took a few risks—nothing much. Everybody does it, but I was unlucky. Suddenly the stock market took a dive."

"What do you mean 'a few risks'?"

He gritted his teeth. "I speculated with clients' money, and now I can't pay it back."

"Oh, God! Parry, you idiot!"

"I know I've been an idiot, Evie, and I swear it'll never happen again if only you'll help me out this time. You wouldn't want to see me in jail, would you?" he pleaded with all his charm.

It was on the tip of her tongue to say it would serve him right, but the old habit of protection was too strong, and she shook her head. "Can't you raise some money against your house?" she asked.

"I've tried that. It's already mortgaged to the hilt."

"What about your Drummond shares? You could sell them."

"Not for that much."

"Suppose I threw in mine as well?"

"Evie, don't you ever read the financial columns?" he asked desperately. "Since your husband announced that there'd be no dividend, the shares have dived. He's made us paupers. But I suppose that doesn't matter to you. I expect he gives you everything you ask for."

Eve smiled, remembering how Luke had lavished gifts on her. For a moment she was distracted, then she looked up to find Parry watching her, his face haggard, and she was instantly contrite. The gulf between her joy and his despair made her feel guilty, even if he had brought his fate on himself. He was Parry, who'd always been her friend and brother, who'd teased her and made her laugh when the world looked black.

"I suppose," Parry said hesitantly, not looking at her, "you wouldn't, I mean, I shouldn't think he remembers everything he's given you—"

"*Parry!* I couldn't even think of selling any of his gifts," she declared, scandalized.

"I'm sorry. I'm sorry," he said quickly. "Don't take any notice of my meanderings, darling. I'm so churned up inside I don't know what I'm saying. Oh, Evie, I'm scared. I have less than a week to make the books balance, and if I can't do it I'll be prosecuted and sent to prison. I can't face that." His voice choked on the last words, and he brushed his hand over his eyes. His tears were perfectly genuine.

Eve drew a long breath. "Don't cry, Parry," she begged. "There *is* something I can do."

"No, it's hopeless," he said huskily. "*He'll* never let you help me. He hates me, Evie. If he knew I was in trouble, he'd enjoy preventing you from rescuing me."

A shadow crossed her face. "Perhaps I'd better not tell him," she said slowly. "I hate deceiving Luke, but...I don't see what else I can do. Look, don't worry. I'll need a few days, but I'm sure I can raise the money." She reached across the table to take his hand in a comforting clasp. "And it'll be our secret."

The sight of Eve's car gave Luke's heart a painful lurch when he arrived back that evening. She was home then. Marcus Laine had called him that afternoon, ostensibly about business but actually to mention lunching at Pipistrello, and whom he'd seen there.

"I know they're related," Marcus had said, "but try to keep Eve away from him. From the way they were holding hands, she's a damned sight too fond of him for her safety and yours."

Now, seeing her car in the garage, he realized how scared he'd been in case she wasn't back yet. He despised himself for the impulse that made him touch the bonnet to see if it were still warm, but he yielded to it nonetheless. To his relief it was cold.

He wondered if she'd tell him she'd rushed off to see Parry on her first day home, and for a dreadful moment he contemplated laying a trap. It would be so easy to ask what she'd been doing, as if he had no idea. Then he pulled himself up firmly. The days of suspicion were over. Eve was his beloved wife, whom he adored and trusted. He'd be as open with her as he knew she'd be with him.

And when he went into the house and saw her smiling at him, all calculation went out of his head. He opened his arms for her to run into, then closed them on her with a profound sense of peace. "I've thought about you all day," he said when he could speak again. "I hurried to get home to you." He kissed her again, then said quickly, "Did you enjoy your gossip with Parry at lunchtime?"

"Yes, thanks," she said, and he told himself it was his imagination that made her voice sound strained. She regarded him quizzically and asked teasingly, "How did you know I'd had lunch with him? Keeping tabs on me?"

"I don't need to. Marcus Laine is the worst old gossip in the city."

"Yes, of course, I saw him there. Parry called me this morning and asked me to lunch. There's nothing to get upset about, darling."

"Who's upset?" he asked cheerfully. "Naturally you want to see him, though I can't say I'm happy about you rushing to meet him on our first day back...." He checked himself. "Forget it. I didn't mean to say that. How is he?"

"He's fine, just fine."

They looked at each other across a chasm. With relief he remembered the gift he'd brought her. "I've got you something," he said, taking a box from his pocket.

"Darling, you buy me too much," she protested, laughing as he turned her to clasp the gold necklace around her neck. She went on exclaiming with determined pleasure in order to fill the silence that might otherwise have fallen, a silence in which Parry's name would have echoed too loudly.

Luke held her a moment, his hands on her shoulders, studying the gleaming metal and trying to resist the thought that he'd been buying her this while she'd been lunching with Parry. *Holding hands?* No, Marcus must have been mistaken about that. "There's no such thing as too much when you love someone as I love you," he said. "I want to give you the world, and even then it wouldn't be good enough for you."

Two days later Eve called Parry. "I've got the money," she said.

"Evie, darling, bless you a thousand times. I can never thank you for this."

"Yes, you can. Don't get into this mess again."

"Of course, of course," he said mechanically. "Where are you?"

"In a phone box in London. I can come straight over and give you a cheque."

He laughed. "Dear trusting Evie. You'd really do it like that, wouldn't you? And suppose I just absconded with your money?"

"You wouldn't cheat an old friend," she said lightly.

"You're right. I wouldn't. But you've got to have security. I insist on that. I've got some arrangements in hand that should take care of everything. Can you be at my house in a couple of hours? I don't want to do this at the office.''

"Can't we make it a bit sooner? I'm meeting Luke and I don't want to be late.''

"An hour and a half. See you.''

But he arrived thirty minutes late and Eve was biting her fingers in impatience. She didn't want to keep Luke waiting and have to say she'd been with Parry. She still thought Tyler had caused Luke's injuries, but she was no longer sure she knew what Parry was capable of. The last few days had shown her that she didn't know him that well, and she felt uncomfortable about having to conceal anything from her husband. She resolved that this was the last time she would meet Parry for a while.

At last his car appeared. Eve could see Parry at the wheel and another man sitting beside him, whom she did not recognize. "Who have you brought with you?'' she asked Parry as he got out of his car.

"My lawyer, of course. He can witness your signature.''

When they were inside, she asked, "Will this take long? Luke's waiting for me.''

"All right, we'll be quick. You can't just give me a cheque for the money, because it would look suspicious when the books are audited. I've got to be able to account for it. The simplest thing is for you to become a client of the firm and receive some shares for your money. We then transfer these to...''

He went on talking, explaining in great detail, and to Eve it all sounded like a merry-go-round. "Do stockbrokers chase their own tails like this all the time?'' she demanded in comical dismay.

He grinned. "I'm afraid so.''

"But you said this was the simplest way.''

"It is. All the others are worse.''

"All right. Let's get on with it."

Parry signaled to the lawyer who produced some papers out of his briefcase. "These are the share transfer forms," Parry explained. "You sign these first, then these, then these..."

She signed hurriedly, and the lawyer countersigned. "Is that it?' she asked at last.

"That's the lot. Evie, I don't know how to thank you."

"Skip it," she said tensely. "I must rush."

She reached Luke's office just as he was looking at his watch impatiently. "Sorry," she said. Before he could ask any questions, she added, "Let's hurry home."

She'd told him no lies, but she had a crushing sense of guilt that made it hard for her to talk on the way home. Luke took her hand and brushed his lips against it, then pulled across the glass that shut them off from the chauffeur and took her into his arms.

Eve felt his lips warm against hers and sensed the eager passion just below the surface, passion that she knew would overwhelm her that night, inciting her own to meet it. In the dark they would become one in the sweet, blissful union that was death and rebirth. But tonight the union would be flawed because she was hiding something from him.

She put her heart and soul into her answering kiss, trying to tell him silently that she loved him despite doing what would make him angry if he knew. But he must never know. And suddenly she felt the true width of the chasm that divided them.

Why can't I talk to you? she thought desperately. Why can't you understand? Why can't I be exactly what you want? Oh, Luke, my darling... forgive me.

Eight

Mrs. Allardyce came into Luke's office and sat down. "I'll start with the bad news," she said. "Parry Drummond is smiling again. The word on the grapevine is that he somehow managed to meet all his obligations." She knew of her employer's enmity toward Parry, although not the cause. To her surprise Luke merely shrugged now.

"Any idea how he raised the cash?" he asked casually.

"I'm afraid not. My banking contact says every finance house for a hundred miles refused to lend him a penny. He seems to have found a private Father Christmas."

"So he conned some poor innocent? That might prove useful later. Keep your ear to the ground." But Luke spoke mechanically. His happiness with Eve had driven vengeful thoughts to the back of his mind. "You said that was the bad news," he remembered. "Does that mean there's some good?"

"Yes. As you instructed, I've also been keeping a watch on the jewelry market, and if you're quick you can have first refusal of a really fabulous diamond collection that's just become available. There's a necklace, a bracelet, earrings, a ring and an aigrette."

Luke grinned. "I don't mind showing my ignorance. What the hell is an aigrette?"

"It's a spray of jewels worn in the hair." She produced a photograph that showed the diamond collection spread out on a black velvet background. Luke whistled and stared at them, while Mrs. Allardyce watched him, trying to reconcile this genial, easygoing man with the grim, slightly satanic employer she was used to. Luke looked up, caught her gaze and laughed aloud. "It's the effect of marriage," he said, correctly interpreting her expression. A rare impulse to mischief made him add, "You should give it another try."

"No, thank you," she said primly. "Once was *quite* enough. Shall I tell the jeweler you're interested?"

"Tell him I want them delivered today."

"The price is three hundred thousand pounds."

"Call him now."

He secured the collection that day and took it home with him. He felt pleased with himself. Although he'd already showered Eve with gifts, he thought of them as mere trinkets. This was the one he'd secretly been searching for, the one that would top everything else.

He found her in their bedroom, reading a book about painting. It was a hot day and she was sitting in her slip, a delicate garment that was cut very low and whose thin material revealed that she wore nothing beneath it. He imagined her pleasure at the gift, how she'd put her arms around him and show her gratitude in actions, and the thought made his blood pound so strongly that he nearly took her in his arms at once and postponed the giving until later.

But, like a child longing for a treat, he couldn't wait to see the delight on her face, and he said at once, "I've bought you a wedding present."

"Another one!" she exclaimed, laughing. "You've bought me four already."

"They were just makeshift. This is the real one. Get ready for a big surprise."

She laughed tenderly at his expression. "All right, I'm ready."

He watched her face eagerly as she opened the box and detected the split second of frozen stillness before she reacted. "Oh, Luke, they're beautiful!" she exclaimed. "But you shouldn't spoil me like this. I have so many lovely things. I don't need more."

"But I need to give you more," he said eagerly. "I want the world to understand that no woman was ever loved as you are."

"You don't have to give me diamonds for that," she said quickly. "Just give me your heart, Luke. That's all I want."

He kissed her. "You have that a thousand times over, but only you and I know about it. Everyone will know about these."

"But why must everyone know?"

"Because I want them to," he said stubbornly. "What's wrong with showing people that I love you?"

"Nothing, but . . ."

He was fitting the necklace about her slender neck, stroking the soft skin with loving fingers as he did so. "The trouble with you," he teased her, "is that you still see me as one of the servants. But I've come a long way, my darling, and I can afford to give you whatever I want to."

Her eyes met his in the mirror. She had a strange expression. "Is that why you gave me these," she asked, "to prove how far you've come?"

"Eve, what is this? I thought you'd be pleased and all you can do is criticize."

"I am pleased," she said valiantly. "I think it's the loveliest gift any woman was ever given."

But it was too late. The moment was gone. He'd looked forward to laying his treasure at her feet, and now she'd spoiled it. Pain made him snap at her. "It damned well ought to be for what it cost."

He regretted the words the moment they were out, but he stubbornly refused to back down. The faint chill on Eve's face enraged him further. "All right, you don't have to say it," he growled. "That was vulgar of me, wasn't it? Well, I *am* vulgar. That's how I made my money. I see what I want and I go for it straight out. I don't spring in the dark like your elegant cousin. I attack from the front and I attack hard, because I'm common and coarse and vulgar. So what? You've always known what I was."

"Luke, please . . . I wasn't going to say anything."

"Not in words, perhaps. But that faint lift of your eyebrows said it all. That's how a *lady* registers disapproval, isn't it?" He knew he should stop this at once, but bitter disappointment made him lash out. "And you're very much a *lady*, Eve." He made the word sound like an insult.

Her face was pale as she began to strip off the necklace from around her throat. "Leave it there!" he commanded. "I'm vulgar enough to want you to show off what I give you."

"And I'm too much of a *lady* to want to," she flashed back, using his own tone. "I'm not a showcase for your wealth. I'm your wife. I want to be loved, not decorated for display. I'd sooner have the cheapest flower in the world as long as you'd gone to buy it yourself. What did these cost you in effort, Luke? A phone call? Or did Miss Allardyce even do that for you?"

He stood in silence while she pulled off the bracelet and packed everything back into the box. When she finished she turned to him, expecting more hostility, but instead she saw a hurt bewilderment on his face that went straight to her heart. Instinctively she opened her arms to him, but he didn't come to her, almost as though he was afraid she would strike him.

"Don't look like that," she said softly. "I love you."

"Do you?" He stayed motionless, looking at her.

Unable to bear his pain, she went to him and slipped her arms about his neck. At first he didn't move, but she wasn't going to let him get away with that, and she pressed her lips against his, putting all her heart into seducing him.

Luke felt what she was doing, and his bitter resentment made him try to resist her. But almost at once he knew it was impossible. The subtle caresses of her lips were pure witchcraft, casting a spell over him so that despite himself the blood began to pound in his veins.

"Don't fight me, Luke," she whispered. "I want you."

She traced the outline of his mouth with her tongue, and the touch of the flickering tip made him tremble. She knew what to do to him. A hundred lovings had taught her that it was the light, soft movements that destroyed his control. He parted his lips, gasping, and she inserted her tongue between them.

His desire for her, never far below the surface, surged up in response, mocking him with the knowledge that she could do what she liked with him and entice him back to her bed with a crook of her little finger. She was kissing him intently, drawing her tongue in leisurely movements over the inside of his mouth, teasing him to challenge her. He took hold of her and felt her naked flesh beneath the thin silk of her slip. Her perfumed body was warm to the touch, and he groaned as the bittersweet sensation invaded him, turning his insides to water.

"Let it happen, Luke," she whispered. "Feel how good it can be for both of us."

She pulled open his shirt and slid her long fingers inside, caressing his chest. *"Eve,"* he said in torment.

"Yes, my love. What do you want me to do?"

"Just keep on with what you're doing," he rasped.

Before the words were out of his mouth, she was removing his shirt. He resisted the impulse to strip and stood motionless, letting her undress him. She did so with delicate skill, making each gesture an allurement, as if it were her own clothes she was removing. When his shirt was gone, she let her fingers drift to the zipper of his trousers, all the while kissing his chest, caressing him with soft movements of her lips. "Eve..." he groaned again, half out of his mind.

He helped her remove the rest of his clothes, and when he was naked his arousal was uncompromisingly evident. He put his arms around her and began to draw her slip up with his fingertips until he could pull it over her head, revealing the sheer magnificence of her form.

He tried to tell himself that all this beauty was his, but in his heart he knew that even now, when she was seducing him, her secret self lived apart. The yielding of her body was an illusion, masking the truth that her spirit had never yielded. She'd claimed the right to her secrets, and now he was married to a woman he couldn't fathom. He could only love her helplessly. Then that thought was swallowed up in the feelings that her fingers were eliciting as they worked intimately on him. Shudders of delight racked his body at her expert enchantment.

At last she drew him to the bed and lay down, pulling him on top and inviting him into her. He claimed her hurriedly, hoping to find in the union of their flesh the secret of whatever she was holding back from him. But somehow everything was different. Instead of being two halves of one person, reunited, they were two people again, and looking down into her face, he saw that she knew it, too. "What is it?" he asked urgently. "Tell me what's wrong."

She smiled, and it was quite different from the hazy, languorous smiles she'd given him at other times, when the happiness of being one with him had touched her very soul. This smile was too bright, as was the voice in which she said, "There's nothing wrong. Nothing." And he stared at her dismayed, knowing she'd told the first lie of their marriage.

Suddenly she clasped him to her. He tried to believe it was because the pleasure was mounting, and not because she wanted to hide her face. Then everything dissolved in an explosion of sensation, giving them, for a fleeting moment, the illusion that their shared passion was enough to solve all problems.

But as they lay together afterward he felt the illusion slip away. He'd thought that once Eve was his he'd never know loneliness again. Now, cradling her in his arms in the aftermath of love, he discovered he was wrong.

Desire had swept away their quarrel but not resolved it. Neither spoke of it in the days that followed, but inwardly both were tense.

It was a couple of weeks later that Luke said, "I want to give a formal dinner at Drummond Lea so that you can meet all my associates."

"I thought I met them that weekend," she said, smiling.

"We weren't married then. You were one of the guests. This time you'll preside, and I'll be so proud of you." He kissed her. "And just to please you I'll even invite Parry."

She laughed. "Bless you."

She set to work, planning and consulting with the cook, work which she enjoyed, for despite her lack of culinary skill she was a gifted hostess. She even purchased a new dress, not because she wanted one, but because she knew Luke would like it, and she was grateful to him for relenting in his hostility to Parry.

She bought the dress on the last day before the dinner and showed it off to Luke in the evening. It was white silk, cut low to show off her graceful arms and neck, and he whistled with admiration. "If I did what I'd like to do right now, it would ruin that dress," he said with a grin.

"You wouldn't risk spoiling it if you knew what it cost," she teased.

But he only shrugged and said, "Who cares if it makes you look like that? It's the perfect setting for your diamonds. You can give them their first outing."

"Oh, no," she said quickly. "I don't want to risk them. They ought to be locked in a vault in London."

"They will be, afterward, but I want you to wear them tomorrow night. I don't buy you gifts to hide away. We're not going to have this argument again, are we?"

"No, but . . . I have several other jewels that are more suitable. Those sapphires you gave me—"

"The diamonds are better," he said stubbornly. He tried to make light of it to cover the aching pit of dismay that had opened within him. "Don't forget that these men will be business associates. If a wife isn't dripping with jewels like a chandelier, people think her husband's not doing too well. It's all part of the performance we put on for each other. You surely don't object to playing your part?"

Eve hesitated, but before she could protest again she saw the hard look in her husband's eyes. "Of course I'll wear them," she said with a sigh. "I just didn't want to take risks with your present."

"I wish I felt that was all it was, Eve," he said softly. "I should hate to think you were ashamed of me." He walked out before she could answer.

Luke was known as an unemotional man, and his runaway marriage had made a sensation. No one wanted to miss seeing him and Eve together, so there were no refusals. On the following evening Eve was waiting to receive fifty guests. She wore the full set of diamonds, including the aigrette set into her swept-up hair. Their splendor set off her blond beauty, and to Luke's eyes she outshone every other woman.

And yet something was missing in the atmosphere. It might be connected with the telephone call Eve had made that afternoon, the call she'd shut off quickly when she'd heard him coming. Or it might be because of the air of tension that surrounded her almost tangibly. But on what should have been a triumphant night, welcoming people to his elegant home by the side of his beautiful wife, Luke had a miserable sense of unease that couldn't be dispelled.

He tried to ignore his own mood, but it was impossible to ignore his wife's. She was nervous, smiling too brightly, greeting her guests too eagerly. The sound of every newly arriving car made her start. Her eyes would flicker quickly to the door, then to himself. He wanted to take her into his arms and say *"What's wrong. Tell me what's worrying you and I'll make it right."* But he couldn't because thrumming at the bottom of his consciousness was the fear that the real cause of her dread was himself.

And then Parry walked in and Eve's fingers clenched in one convulsive spasm before she went forward, smiling, to welcome him. Luke went with her and forced himself to extend a hand to greet his enemy. He never knew what either of them said or did. What stood out for him with searing clarity was the amusement on Parry's face as he looked at

Eve. His cold, green eyes, so like a snake's, slid over the diamonds adorning her neck and wrists and hair, and behind the polite stretching of the mouth that passed for a smile, Luke knew that Parry was laughing uproariously. But all Parry said was, "They're beautiful, Evie. What did you do? Seduce an oil sheikh?"

"The diamonds were my gift to my wife," Luke said stiffly.

"Of course, of course. No offense meant. Evie knows I'm harmless, don't you, darling?"

Luke clenched his hands, wishing he could sock Parry on the jaw, as much as for his habit of saying "Evie" as for the "darling." He had an unnerving sense that something was inexplicably wrong. Parry was at ease as he hadn't been the last time they met. It might simply be the effect of being relieved of financial care, but Luke had a feeling there was more.

Perry passed on, but not before he'd given the diamonds a last look from eyes glinting with malicious humor and drawled, "Well, well."

"If something amuses you, why don't you share the joke with us?" Luke demanded in a deadly voice.

"The Pattersons are arriving," Eve said quickly. "We must go and say hello."

Alec Patterson was a man Luke disliked and never more so than tonight when he clapped Luke on the back and brayed, "So Eve managed to get back to her old home. Clever girl, Eve. Always said so."

"Are you suggesting that my wife married me to recover her heritage?" Luke asked softly.

"Oh, ah, good Lord, no!" Patterson had spoken from stupidity rather than malice, and he seemed relieved when his wife hurried him away. Luke looked around him and wondered how many of his guests thought the same, and how many of them could see the joke from which he was excluded.

The evening had the slow-moving quality of a nightmare. With one part of his mind he watched himself being the perfect host. With another part he watched Eve. There was never a moment when he wasn't conscious of her, how she looked, who she was talking to. Her sheer loveliness made him ache, yet suspicion pervaded him, poisoning everything, even his love.

At last Parry sighed and said, "Well, I must be off. I've a busy day tomorrow," and it was the signal for a general movement. Eve walked out to the car with him, and Luke resisted the temptation to go, too. He wasn't going to give anyone the satisfaction of thinking he didn't trust his wife. But he was in torment as he waited for her to return, and he talked mechanically, hardly knowing what he said.

He escorted Denzil and Vivienne to their car, and out of the corner of his eye he could see Eve, still talking to Parry. He tried not to listen, but luck was against him, and there was a slight lull in his own conversation, just in time for him to hear Parry laugh and say, "You shouldn't have worried, my pet. I promised not to give you away and I'm a man of my word. I wouldn't queer your pitch when you've handled him so cleverly."

He didn't know how he got through the remaining farewells, but after what seemed an eternity the last guest had gone and they could return to the house.

He followed Eve upstairs, and when the door was firmly closed behind them he said coldly, "Perhaps I should add my congratulations at the clever way you've handled me."

"Luke, don't take any notice of the things Parry says. He ... he can't always be trusted."

"So you've discovered that at last? But it doesn't stop you from conspiring with him against me."

Something desperate in the look she cast him almost made him relent, but he hardened his heart. "I want to know what you made him promise not to tell me. What is it that he finds so funny and why mustn't I be allowed to know? *Tell me*, Eve. It's time there was some truth telling between us."

"All right," she said heavily. "I meant no harm, but perhaps I should tell you everything."

Nine

The trouble began when you bought me these," Eve said, touching the diamonds about her throat. "You see, they used to be mine."

"What do you mean?" he asked. Dimly he perceived that she was saying something appalling, something that would make him want to howl his rage and anguish to the world. But for the moment his mind didn't want to take it in.

"I inherited this diamond set from my mother. Until recently I kept it in a bank vault. But I took it out a few days ago and sold it."

He shook his head as if trying to clear a mist. "I don't understand. If you needed money, why didn't you come to me?"

"I couldn't have done that, knowing how you dislike Parry—"

"What the hell has Parry got to do with it?" he said in a soft, ominous voice.

"I needed the money for him. He was in trouble."

The truth hit Luke like a sledgehammer in the chest. "That was how he paid his debts," he breathed incredulously. "*You* did it. You sold your jewels for him, and then I bought them back for you. No wonder he was laughing."

"I was horrified when you gave them to me. I knew you'd hate it if you ever discovered the truth, but I didn't want to do it, Luke. It was just a dreadful coincidence. And when you insisted on me wearing them tonight, I tried so hard to get out of it. I knew Parry would recognize them. I called him today and begged him to say nothing. I didn't want you to be hurt."

"Didn't want me to . . . ?" He stopped and stared at her as the full import of what had happened dawned on him. "You tricked me," he said slowly. "Right from the very first evening when you came to ask me to declare a dividend because you were penniless. It was all a lie."

She had unclasped the necklace. Now she paused with the glittering gems falling over her hands in a shower. "I never said I was penniless," she protested.

"You said if you'd had any money you wouldn't have come."

"I said I had no *ready cash*," she emphasized. "And that was true. The diamonds were my only asset except for the shares. I didn't want to have to turn them into money. You interpreted my words in the way that suited you. You wanted me to be penniless so that you could have me in your power, but I never said I was. I asked for that dividend as a matter of justice."

"You let me think that you were pleading for yourself," Luke snapped. "But it was for him."

"I couldn't tell you that. I didn't have Parry's permission to discuss his affairs with you. Luke, he's my cousin. I was just doing him an innocent favor."

"And the sale of these?" he demanded sarcastically, holding the necklace up to her. "Was that an 'innocent favor'?"

In her agitation Eve answered without thinking. "I had to help him. He'd been using clients' money. I couldn't let him go to jail, could I?"

As soon as the words were out of her mouth, she knew she shouldn't have said them. In the silence Luke smiled, and it made her blood freeze. "Clients' money?" he repeated slowly. "I didn't know that. I must have slipped up."

Eve stared at him as she realized that he was storing the information up for future use. "Oh, God," she whispered. "What kind of man are you?"

Her horror fanned the flame of anger smoldering inside him. He stared with cruel disillusion at this woman whom he'd worshiped and who'd deceived him to protect his enemy. "I've just realized what kind of man I am, Eve—a credulous clown. I believed in you twice, and the second time I should have known better."

"Luke..."

"It's all clear now," he said, speaking as if in a daze. "Parry's the man you really love. You married me for his sake. He was in my power and you thought if you could keep me besotted with you, you could protect him. You even sold the only thing you had to save his skin."

Eve shook her head in vigorous protest. "I'm not in love with Parry. I know you've got some crazy ideas about him, but—" She broke off with a gasp of alarm as she saw Luke's livid face.

"Crazy ideas!" he raged. "Look at that." He pointed to the scar that stood out against his pallor. "That's not a crazy idea. It's a reality that I live with every day. Just as it's a reality that my wife conspires with the man who did it to me, and now I know why. Tell me, just how much does a woman have to love one man to deceive and cheat another?''

"I never deceived you."

"What about these?" he shouted, snatching up the necklace.

"I couldn't help that," she cried. "Can't you see jewels aren't important?" She began to strip off the ones she was still wearing, tearing the aigrette off so forcefully that her glorious hair fell down around her shoulders. "They're only *things*," she said. "They don't matter."

"Whatever makes you lie to me matters."

"I didn't lie. I just . . . didn't tell you."

"I'm not subtle enough for your moral twists and turns," he said with cold sarcasm. "The difference between 'just not telling' me and conspiring with my enemy is obscure to me. And I might never have found out if I hadn't wanted to please you with a special wedding gift." Anguish swept him at the memory of his own naive pleasure as he'd made his offering. "And you were laughing at me," he choked. "Now he's laughing at me, too, and soon the whole of London will be laughing."

"That's really all you care about," she said bitterly. "You accuse me of not loving you, but it's *you* who don't love me. I'm just a trophy to you, a way of proving you could get the woman you couldn't have years ago. *And that's all I've ever been.*"

"And what have I been to you? A way of protecting your lover!"

"You can't really believe that," she pleaded.

"I believe it," he said.

They looked at each other, strangers. Eve was deathly pale, searching his face for any sign of softening, but finding none. She'd warned him that one day she'd be toppled from her pedestal and his disillusion would make him turn on her. But even she hadn't thought it would come with such terrifying swiftness. "If you really think that of me," she said at last, "we haven't anything left to say to each other. You'd better leave."

He walked out without a word and realized at once that he didn't know where to go. Since their return they hadn't spent a night apart, and he thought of Eve's room as his own. At last he made his way along the corridor to the cell-like room he'd taken over from Tyler. As he entered, its bleakness engulfed him like freezing air, and its loneliness seemed to cry out to his own.

He lay on the hard, narrow bed, staring into the darkness, his tortured mind compulsively reliving the events of the evening. He was haunted by Parry's face, sniggering at the way he and Eve had triumphed. Patterson was there, too, with his snide observation about Eve's cleverness. They'd all been jeering at him enjoying the joke of his love and pride in the wife who was "handling him so cleverly."

His mind went back to the time when he'd brought the diamonds home for her. That had been the start—no, before that. On their first day home she'd slipped off to meet Parry because it was Parry she'd loved all along, even when she was in his arms in Scotland, when he'd thought her most completely his. He put his hands over his face in a silent agony of suffering.

He tried not to think about her and to turn his thoughts to the business of enduring the rest of his life. But that was too bleak to be faced yet. He'd once said to her, "If you aren't good, nothing in the world is good." But she wasn't good, and now the world was chaos.

He wondered what she was doing. Would she telephone Parry to tell him what had happened? Would she go to him? Perhaps he'd get up tomorrow morning to find her gone. The thought caused him to break out in a cold sweat, and he had to hold on to the iron sides of the bed to keep from rushing to her room to make sure she was still there. He didn't release his grip until he was sure he had the temptation under control.

He told himself it didn't matter, anyway. Let her go. It would be the best thing. But he stiffened whenever he heard a noise in the house, and for several hours he lay there, agonizingly alert, until at last he fell into a restless sleep.

He awoke to find himself aching all over. On the way down to breakfast he walked quickly past her room without a look. The table was laid for one, and Mrs. Carter told him that Eve was still in her room. He managed to say, in a voice whose normality surprised him, that she was tired after the previous night and he wouldn't disturb her.

He hadn't seen her by the time he left for town. He worked all day like an automaton and went home late, telling himself that he'd find her gone. But Mrs. Carter told him she'd gone to bed early.

He hesitated outside her door. It would be so easy to go inside and feel the warmth and delight steal over him at the sight of her, to let her smile tell him that nothing mattered but the love they shared. Then he remembered that they shared nothing. She didn't love him. He'd simply been useful. He waited a moment to steady himself against the ache that settled again over his heart after briefly lifting, then walked on.

He returned earlier the next day and found her out riding. He took the chance of going to her room and removing some of his things. There was a dreadful finality about the act. He couldn't see ahead to any future where they could surmount what had come between them and be together again.

He heard her come into the house and up the stairs. After a while there was a knock on his door. "May I come in?" she called.

"If you like."

Her face was very pale, and she looked as if she hadn't slept, but she was calm. "Shouldn't we talk?" she asked.

"If you think there's anything to say, by all means," he replied coldly, not looking at her.

"Luke, I can't believe you really meant some of the things you said the other night. You were angry, and perhaps you had the right to be. I should have told you about those diamonds when you wanted me to wear them, but I didn't realize what was going to happen."

"Didn't realize Parry's attitude would reveal so much, you mean? But he's the type who bites the hand that feeds him. If you weren't so besotted with him, you'd have known that."

"Oh, God, not that again! What can I say to convince you?"

"After what happened, nothing. So let's not discuss it."

"But we can't just leave things like this. There's so much I want to say to you...."

"But I don't want to hear it, Eve," he said bleakly. "There doesn't seem much point."

"Not even to save our marriage?" she asked passionately.

"Do we have a marriage? That's not what I'd call it."

He heard her draw in her breath sharply. "Are you saying you want me to go?" she asked.

"There's no need to be melodramatic," he said coolly to cover the painful jerk of his heart at the mention of her going. "Perhaps you've forgotten we have more guests coming tomorrow."

"Can't we put them off? I don't think I can face people just now."

"Surely that should be my line?" he enquired with an ironic smile that didn't reach his eyes. "I'm the one that was mocked. If I can face people, you certainly can. It'll give you another chance to show off your triumph."

"Don't talk like that," she cried passionately. "Luke, please, stop this before it goes any farther, *before it's too late*."

"Too late for what?" he demanded with soft savagery. "Tell me what you think we have that's worth saving."

She threw out her hands in appeal. "I thought we had love."

"So did I, Eve," he said in a voice of deadly quiet. "So did I."

She let her hands fall and watched him in silence for a moment before going out and closing the door behind her.

Their guests the next evening were Brian and Angela Parker, a middle-aged couple that Luke knew slightly. They hadn't been able to attend the big function that had taken place two days ago. Brian Parker looked like an amiable country doctor, or an absentminded cleric, or anything except what he was, which was a brilliant and successful stockbroker. Luke was planning to do more business with him and found him personally engaging.

A few minutes before the Parkers were due to appear he went to the door of Eve's room. After hesitating indecisively for a second, he raised his hand to knock. But the door opened at once and she appeared in time to see what he'd been about to do. It was the first time he'd ever knocked at her door, and she gave him a wry smile. "Will I do?" she asked.

"You look perfect, as always," he returned politely.

They descended the stairs together, knowing that the pattern had been set for the evening. For tonight there'd be a truce. They'd smile and laugh and even speak to each other amiably, but beneath the surface nothing had changed.

Luke liked Angela Parker, a cheerful, plump woman who could make him laugh, and under other circumstances he would have enjoyed the evening. But tonight he was on edge as the kindly Parkers toasted him and his bride, and the two of them had to pretend to be blissfully happy. No one, he thought, could have guessed the frozen wasteland between them.

Eve virtually monopolized Brian. While seeming to concentrate on Angela, Luke managed to overhear a good deal of his wife's conversation. Brian was talking about stockbroking, and at first Luke was inclined to pity Eve, who had no more than a moderate interest in business, but then he realized that she was questioning him in an unusually persistent manner. Brian was expanding happily under his hostess's attention, but Luke had a disconcerting sensation of something strange going on. Angela had to tap him on the arm to recall his attention. "Sorry," he said hastily.

"Oh, my dear, I can't blame you for not being able to take your eyes off her," Angela said generously. "She's glorious, isn't she?" She sighed. "When I was a girl I used to dream about being like Eve."

"She's certainly very attractive," Luke agreed in a strained tone.

"Heavens, what a cold fish you sound! It's a great deal more than being attractive. She has something that only one woman in a million has. It's not just beauty or charm or even sex appeal, although heaven knows Eve has them all in abundance. It's an extra 'something' that can cause men to fall in love to order and make utter fools of themselves."

She chuckled comfortably. "It's lucky I'm the only one who knows how to keep Brian's feet warm at night, or I'd be getting jealous at the way he's looking at her."

She spoke without rancor, for she was the most amiable soul alive and would have been horrified to know that her sincere admiration of Eve had lodged like an arrow in Luke's heart.

At the end of the evening Luke and Eve stood on the steps waving goodbye to the Parkers. For the sake of appearances he put an arm around her bare shoulders and felt the shock of contact with her warm skin. It was soft to the touch, and with dismay he felt the old, treacherous delight begin to invade him. As soon as the car disappeared, he snatched his hand away, trying to tell himself that he was imagining things. He didn't *want* to want her. She'd betrayed him, not with her body but with her mind and heart, and he must never fall into her snares again. But how could he stick to that hard resolve when the mere feel of her flesh against his hand could send his blood rioting and dancing through his veins, and his senses aching with desire?

He returned to the living room and quickly poured himself a brandy. "I'll have one, too," Eve said, coming in behind him.

He handed her the glass. "You were the perfect hostess tonight," he remarked ironically. "A little neglectful of Angela perhaps, but Brian had nothing to complain about."

"Nor Angela," Eve observed lightly. "I gave her the chance to flirt with you, and I don't suppose she minded that at all. Actually Brian and I were talking about his firm."

"So I heard. You were asking some very knowledgeable questions. I didn't know you even knew that much about stockbroking."

"I've been reading some books..." she began hesitantly.

"Why bother? You've always given me the impression that you disliked business."

"Perhaps it's time I stopped disliking it." She spoke with an attempt at lightness, but it seemed to Luke that she had trouble finding the words. He stared at her, puzzled. "I mean," Eve continued awkwardly, "I didn't realize how fascinating it could be, and there are a lot of things I want to ask you—"

"Oh, no, Eve, please stop this!" he broke in urgently. "Believe me, there's no need for it and it doesn't help."

"I...don't understand."

"Don't you? I believe it's known as 'taking an interest' in your husband's work?" He added ironically, "The perfect recipe for a happy marriage."

"Is that what you think I'm doing?" she asked, looking at him curiously.

"What else? You never even pretended to care about business before and I actually respected you for that. You were your own woman, living your own life. But now..." He frowned and rubbed his eyes as if trying to shift the weariness. "I know you mean well, but please let's skip it."

"All right," she said in a colorless voice, "if that's how you feel, I can't say any more."

She set down her glass and turned as if to go. She was very close to him, the golden lamplight burnishing her skin. He smelled the warm, musky odor of her perfume and his head reeled. "Angela was admiring you tonight," he said, to stop her leaving. "She said you had the gift of making men fall in love to order."

Eve smiled ironically. "I never managed that with you."

His blood was pounding, making it difficult to speak. "You've always done as you like with me. You know that. Do you think you couldn't still?"

She gave a mirthless laugh. "Oh, yes, I can make you want me. That much is easy."

She took a step closer and reached up to touch his cheek with soft fingers that sent forks of fire through him, then pulled his head down until his lips were against hers. "I can make you want me, Luke. All I have to do is this..." She caressed his lips with her own. "And this." She let her tongue flicker in and out of his mouth, the brief contact leaving him trembling with desire.

Inwardly he gave a silent groan as he realized how truly Angela had spoken when she'd said Eve could persuade men to make "utter fools" of themselves. He could see his own foolishness and he was helpless to do anything about it.

"I can make you mad for me, Luke," she continued with a strange inflection in her voice that might almost have been sadness. "I know all the right things to do because I know just what you like. But I wonder how much it means."

"It might... mean a great deal," he said thickly, despising himself. "Must we ask questions?" He wanted to drown in her and blot out the questions and the fears.

"Yes, because the answers matter. Is this all you want of me?" She was kissing him again as she spoke, caressing his face. Her fingertips briefly touched his scar.

Suddenly he stiffened, wrenching back and staring down into her face, his own face livid. Pain seemed to explode in his head where she'd touched him, as though he'd felt, not her gentle fingers, but the heavy fist that had caused his injury. A red mist swam before his eyes. He burned again with the bruises and lacerations of his smashed face, heard Parry's giggle of pleasure and saw Megan's shock and grief before she collapsed, her eyes full of love in her last hours as she fought to communicate with him. That was what Parry had done, and Eve had allied herself with him.

"Yes," he said in a deadly cold voice. "Yes, Eve, that's all I want of you, because I now see that it's all you've ever offered. We made a neat bargain. Neither of us has anything to complain about."

He could have laughed to think how easily he'd been caught in her trap again. She'd even given him a kind of warning, so sure of her power that she could boast of it at the very moment she was exerting her spell. But he was wiser now. He pushed her away and spoke coldly. "Don't touch me again. Keep away from me. I can't endure the sight of you."

He turned away sharply. Eve stood where she was, watching him with an expression of love and heartbreak that he never saw. Everything in her passionately denied that their marriage could die like this, although it was cruelly obvious. She longed to find the words for one last appeal that would break down the barriers of pride and suspicion guarding his heart! Then perhaps he would look at her again with the old love in his eyes. He would take her in his arms, and she could tell him of the hideous fear that had grown in her over the past few days, a fear that she was trapped in a terrifying situation, from which only he could rescue her.

The silence between them went on and on, and there was only his broad, unyielding back. At last he turned and her hands flew to her mouth at the sight of his face, for it bore the look she'd dreaded to see. She knew now that it was hopeless. There was no yielding in that harsh face, no forgiveness or understanding. And there never would be.

"Then I'll go," she said, struggling for composure. "You're not the only one who can't endure. I've watched you, these past few days, growing more and more like Tyler. I've tried not to believe it because I know what he was—

hard, ruthless and unforgiving. And I wouldn't face how deeply you're his son. But your heritage shows, Luke, and it's going to show more in the years to come. I don't want to be there to see it."

Out of sight he clenched a fist. He'd told himself many times that their marriage was finished, but he hadn't been able to say it. Now she'd said it herself and instead of relief a storm of misery shook him. But the only words that would come gave no hint of his feelings. "Nonetheless you *will* be there," he grated. "Do you think I'm going to be mocked because my bride walked out on me? Parry would love that, wouldn't he? And how long would it take him to spread the story of how you jilted me once before—with his help, of course—and how the two of you deluded me again. Do you imagine I'm going to stand for that?"

Eve brushed a hand over her face, leaving just a trace of tears on her cheeks. "If that's all you care about, the sooner I leave the better." Her voice rose to a cry of pain. "I warned you not to marry me, Luke. I told you I wasn't a goddess—only a fallible woman—but you wouldn't listen. You only wanted me to fulfil some preconceived dream of your own, and I can't do it. I'm not an angel who can rewrite the past for you. I'm a woman who loves you and who could have made the future happy. But you didn't want that because you're so wrapped up in hate and the desire for revenge that there's no place in your heart for what I have to give."

"The only thing you have to give doesn't concern my heart or yours," he said cruelly. "It's something much more basic and easily negotiated. We fixed the price and now I'm holding you to the contract. You'll stay with me, Eve, because I say so and because you can't survive in the world out there without my money—unless you have any other assets you didn't tell me about."

"No," she said, very pale. "That diamond set was all I possessed."

He nodded. "You gave Parry all you possessed and you expect me to believe your relationship is innocent? I've been your dupe, but I'm not that much of a dupe." His voice grew very hard. "Listen to me. As far as I'm concerned, this subject is closed. We're married and that's how we're going to stay. I'll be a conscientious husband who'll give you the best of everything, and I'm sure you'll be the very model of a perfect wife. My colleagues will all say how lucky I am." He paused, trying not to look at her stricken face, and drew a painful breath. "In time I dare say we'll both get used to it," he finished heavily.

There was a dreadful silence. Then Eve turned and left the room. He watched her climb the stairs, and after a moment he heard her door close and the key turn in the lock. He discovered that he was aching all over from tension and that his limbs were trembling.

He saw no sign of Eve when he went down the following morning. When he returned from work that night, he found her gone. She had left behind every stitch of clothing he'd ever given her, and every piece of jewelry, including the diamonds. There was no letter.

Ten

There's a man called Sanders to see you," Grace Allardyce said. "He looks like a disreputable type, but he says he has an appointment."

"Show him in," Luke commanded curtly, ignoring the unspoken question.

The man who came through the office door did indeed look disreputable, not because of his clothes, which were snappy enough, but because of a certain personal seediness that no amount of good dressing could hide. He presented Luke with his card: Sanders: Private Investigator. "You wanted to see me?" he said, sitting down without waiting to be asked.

"I have a job for you," Luke said frigidly. "When we talked on the telephone you said you specialized in financial investigations."

"I have people working for me who can find out anything you want to know—fraudulent transactions, Swiss bank account numbers, you name it."

"The man I'm interested in is hardly likely to have a Swiss bank account," Luke observed dryly.

"You mean he's honest?" Sanders asked, sounding baffled.

"I mean he's broke. By how much? That's the point." Luke passed one of Parry's business cards across the desk. Sanders studied it and nodded as though the name was known to him. "I want everything you can discover about his debts—how much, how pressing. In particular I'm interested in his tendency to speculate with his clients' funds. He did it before and nearly got caught, but he managed to cover himself in time."

"And when he does it again you want to be ready to pounce," Sanders commented.

Luke compressed his lips in displeasure. "Just find out what he's up to and you'll be well paid," he observed curtly.

When Sanders had left, Grace came in without waiting to be called. She had a bank statement in her hand. "That cheque still hasn't been cashed," she said.

"She sent it back," Luke said bleakly.

Grace hesitated. Luke trusted her completely, and she was privy to all his secrets, but in the three months since Eve had left him his uncertain temper had made even her cautious. "Perhaps Mrs. Harmon has some money of her own," she suggested.

"She has nothing," Luke said savagely. "Unless . . ." He was assailed again by the hideous suspicion that Eve might be taking money from Parry. He'd often tried to push the thought aside, but somehow she was managing without Luke's help, for every cheque he'd sent her had been returned.

He got to his feet suddenly, feeling as if he were being driven by demons. "I'm going out," he said.

"But you have an appointment in ten minutes," she protested.

"Cancel it!" he said, halfway out the door.

He drove in search of Oakapple Street, where Eve now lived. The name meant nothing to him, for he knew little of the outskirts of London. As the expensive part of town fell away, he stopped and checked again, sure that there must be some mistake. But he found he was headed in the right direction.

The environment grew steadily shabbier until he found himself in a depressingly squalid neighborhood with many houses boarded up. Luke had a sinking feeling of dismay at the thought of Eve in these surroundings.

At last he found Oakapple Street. Despite its name, it had no trees and was lined with large houses, divided into flats, that looked as if they'd known better days long ago. Luke stopped outside one of them and surveyed it. It had three floors and an attic apartment. Paint was peeling from the sides, and even from where he was parked he could see that one of the windows was badly warped and had been tied shut with colored string.

"Eve," he murmured, "was I such a monster that you were driven to this?"

He left his car and went up the steps to consult the list of tenants. He knew she lived in flat 4, which seemed to be the attic, but beside the bell he found the name E. Chadwick. He frowned, wondering where he'd heard the name before. Then it came to him. Eve's mother had been Chadwick before her marriage.

His wife had rejected even his name. Luke hadn't thought that anything could still hurt, but this brought a sharp pain that took him by surprise. He gritted his teeth and pressed

the bell. There was no response, so he rang again, leaning
close to the door to catch any sound, but there was total silence.

"It ain't working."

Luke turned to see the owner of the belligerent voice that
had come from behind him. He found a large, sullen-
looking woman in her fifties, standing in the street, regard-
ing him with the grim pleasure of one who had bad news to
impart. "It ain't worked for ages," she informed him, adding in case he hadn't got the point, "So it's no use ring-
ing."

"Then how does anyone ever call?" Luke enquired.

"No one does. That's 'ow she likes it."

"You mean she has no visitors?" he asked with a painful
spasm of hope. He despised himself for the question, but he
needed relief from the misery that tormented him whenever
he thought of Eve and Parry.

"Ain't that what I just said? No one calls and no one
phones."

"How do you know no one phones her?" Luke asked.

"'Cause she ain't got a phone," the woman said with the
air of one explaining to an idiot. "Not that she could afford it, 'cause she ain't got a penny to bless herself with. She
usually pays the rent late, though I always get it in the end,
that I will say," she added generously.

"You're her landlady?"

"I own the place. My name's Mrs. Thompson."

"Can you let Miss Chadwick know that I'm here,
please?"

"Oh, that's nice! *Me* traipsing all the way up them
stairs?" she said in outrage. "What do you think I am?"

She fitted her key into the lock and opened the front door.
Luke slipped adroitly in behind her. "Then I'll just go up,"
he said.

The stairs seemed to grow gloomier as he climbed higher, as though the house were progressively abandoning hope. As he reached the last step, he tripped and steadied himself on the wall. He felt for the wall switch. Overhead a naked bulb came on and by its dim light he made out a scuffed place in the linoleum. His blood ran cold as he thought of Eve catching her foot and falling down the steep stairs.

He raised his hand to knock on the door in front of him, then hesitated. Now that the moment had come he was suddenly afraid. He didn't know exactly what it was he feared, unless it was the distant look that he'd seen in her eyes at their last meeting, which had wounded him as nothing else could have done.

He drew in his breath sharply and told himself not to weaken. It was he who had the right to be angry. His wife had deceived him, not the other way around. If he let her think he'd come here as a suppliant, she would walk over him whenever she pleased. He set his face in hard lines of pride and knocked firmly on the door.

He heard her light step, then the door swung open and she stood before him. She was dressed in jeans and a shirt. An artist's paintbrush was in her hand, and she had a faraway look, as though he'd disturbed her in the middle of something absorbing and her mind was still elsewhere. Then her eyes focused and something that might have been gladness flickered in them. But it died and was replaced with wariness when she saw his face more clearly.

They looked at each other, and the terrible things they'd said fell like shadows between them. Her face was different in a way he couldn't define, as if every feature had grown more vivid. "Hello, Luke," she said.

"I thought I ought to see how you were," he said stiffly.

"That was very conscientious of you. Won't you come in?"

She stood back to let him pass and he went through. The front door led directly into what he guessed was the main room. It was well lit by the high mansard windows, but the light only showed up the general shabbiness. The carpet was threadbare, the upholstery worn through and one corner of the armchair was held up by a pile of books. "Dear God!" he breathed. "What on earth do you think you're doing here?"

"It's almost impossible to find anywhere to rent in London," she said with a shrug. "I was very lucky to get it."

"Lucky?" He gave a grim laugh. "I call it perverse to live in a dump like this when you don't have to."

"But I do have to."

"You have a perfectly good home waiting for you," he said coldly. "Your proper place is there."

"With a husband who can't endure the sight of me?"

"I said a lot of hasty things," he said impatiently. "We both did. There's no need to remember them now. I'm willing to have you come back." He hadn't meant to put it like that, but pride and hurt were chaining his tongue.

Eve gave a little ironic smile. "That's very generous of you, Luke."

He reddened, knowing how pompous he'd sounded. Surely she could see that he hadn't meant it like that? But her eyes were coolly amused, making him feel like a clumsy oaf. Embarrassment made him snap, "I can't afford to have people knowing that my wife lives likes this."

"No one knows I'm your wife. I'm living under my mother's name."

"Yes, I saw. But why?"

"It's the only name that's honestly mine. I'm not a Drummond. That was just Tyler's way of spiting you, and I can't use your name, Luke, because I don't feel like your wife. In a strange way I never really did. Our time together was beautiful, but I realize now that there was always something unreal about it.''

He was silent. If he'd spoken, his voice would have betrayed how profoundly her words had affected him.

"I'm sorry. I should have asked you to sit down," she said, as she would have done to any stranger. "I was just going to make some coffee."

She went into the tiny kitchen and he followed. As she busied herself with cups, he noticed something on her left hand. "What's this?" he demanded, taking hold of her wrist to study the angry red mark.

"It's nothing." She tried to take her hand away, but he held on to it.

"It looks like a burn."

"I spilt a little hot milk, that's all."

He grimaced wryly. "You once said you were no good in a kitchen."

Then he wished he hadn't spoken. It brought back memories of Scotland and the bliss they'd shared there. He stared at the burn, which must have been a nasty injury when it was new. The thought of her enduring pain in this bleak place, trying to care for herself alone, made him thrust her hand sharply away, turning from her so that she shouldn't see his face.

After a while he looked back to find her at work again. He watched her, trying to get used to the way she looked. He'd seen her casually dressed before, as a young girl, and when they were in Scotland. But it had been the kind of casualness that only money could buy. The clothes she had on now must have been bought at a jumble sale. The faded jeans hugged her hips tightly, and Luke suddenly realized that she'd lost weight.

Now he knew why her face had seemed different. Her high, beautiful cheekbones could be discerned more clearly under the flesh, and the lines of her curved mouth were more perfectly defined. He'd always thought of Eve as an earthy woman. Sensuality glowed through every line of her body, and the joyous carnality they'd shared had seemed a confirmation. Now he saw something spiritual about her face, something shining from her large eyes.

She wore no makeup and she was too pale, except for the dark smudges under her eyes, as if she hadn't slept. He knew an irrational anger that his beautiful Eve should have come to this. And yet she seemed to him more maddeningly attractive now than at any time since he'd known her. Fear swept him as he thought how easy it would be to yield to the temptation to take that frail body into his arms and caress it with tender passion. "You're too thin," he said roughly. "Haven't you been eating properly?"

"I eat plenty," she said. "Here, what are you doing?" Luke had begun to open cupboards, his lips tightening as he saw how little was inside. "I haven't been out to shop yet," she said, quickly. "Please go away. This is a tiny kitchen."

He walked out and picked up her purse, emptied the contents into his hand and was surveying them as she returned with the coffee. "How dare you!" she said furiously. "You had no right to touch my purse."

"It's good that I did or I wouldn't have known the truth," he said grimly. "How are you going to buy food with this?" He held out the little money he'd discovered.

"I shall get some from the bank."

"And how much have you got in there? Four pence?"

"That's none of your business," she cried.

"It's my business if my wife starves to death!" he shouted.

"But I'm not your wife anymore...if I ever was."

"What is that supposed to mean?"

"Oh, Luke, let's have the truth at last," she said wearily. "You never loved me. You just wanted to reclaim me. You once told me that you never let yourself be permanently worsted, that however long it took, you always evened the score. And that's all our marriage was to you, even if you didn't realize it. You wanted to dress me up and drape me in jewels, but you never looked at the woman underneath. If you had, none of this would come as a surprise to you." She indicated the room with a sweep of her arm. "You can't imagine how I can live without luxury, can you? You probably thought Parry was supporting me."

"If I did, I don't believe it anymore," he said gruffly. "I wonder now if he's given you any help at all since he broke up your marriage."

"It wasn't Parry who broke us up. It was something else, something that was all wrong from the start. If it helps you to know it, I haven't seen him since I left you. You can believe that or not, as you like."

"I do believe it. Are you saying he hasn't even offered you his help, after what you did for him?"

"It doesn't matter. Can't you understand that? I don't need his help any more than I need yours. I can survive alone. I prefer it that way. For the first time in my life I'm not struggling to conform to someone else's view of me. Tyler tried to turn me into a Drummond, David wanted me to be his handmaiden and you wanted me to be a goddess. Now I don't have to pretend to be any of those things, and it's like a weight lifted from my shoulders."

"But how are you living?"

"I have my work. It doesn't earn much, but it makes me happy and it keeps me independent."

She indicated the window beside which stood an easel with a small picture. Luke looked at it, frowning. "You did this?"

"No, it's a couple of hundred years old. I'm restoring it for an auction house. I do free-lance work for them, small pictures, vases, that kind of thing."

He knew nothing about art, but he recalled the absorption on her face when she'd opened the door, and he studied the picture blankly, trying to find some clue. A small desk stood nearby and his eye fell on a letter with a cheque attached. "Is this all they pay you?" he demanded. "You couldn't buy a meal in a decent restaurant for that."

"I earned it honestly and not as a kept woman," she told him proudly.

He paled. "Is that all you were with me?" he asked harshly. "A kept woman?"

"That's all it felt like sometimes," she said with a sad smile. "We shouldn't have married, Luke. We'd changed too much. I can remember when an amount like this would have been a fortune to you. I loved the man you were then. But now you've become a monster, not in your face, but in your heart."

He could think of nothing to say.

"You think I'm mad to live like this," she went on, "but I have something you don't understand, and I don't think I could ever explain it to you."

"You could come home and still have all this," he said gruffly. "Do whatever you like. I won't stop you."

"It wouldn't work, Luke. I've returned to the things of real beauty. I don't want to get sucked back into all that meaningless glitter."

"And what we had...was that meaningless?" Luke demanded harshly.

"I don't know what we had, or if we had anything. I thought once that you loved me—"

"Damn you, stop tormenting me," he swore. "You know I'm mad about you."

"Yes, you're mad about me, but you don't *love* me. You don't even see the difference, do you?"

Unable to answer this he asserted, "You're still my wife and I'm going to keep you."

"It's too late for that. Whatever we might have had is dead."

He took a step toward her. "We both thought that once before and we found out we were wrong. What's between us will never die, and you know it, however hard you try to deny it. Do you think I couldn't make you want me as much as ever?"

She took a step back from him. "I know you could, but don't you see that wanting isn't loving?"

His face set in a look of stubborn determination. "Then we'll have to make it do," he said, and pulled her into his arms.

She felt so fragile that for a moment his heart misgave him, but immediately caution was swept away as the old magic began to work again, sending heat flowing through him, melting his bones. Her lips were wine and honey. She was Eve, and he wanted her enough to forget everything else, including his bitterness and distrust of her. In her slim, trembling body he knew he could find Eden, if only briefly.

Her hands were flat against his chest, but she wasn't fighting him. She seemed dazed by what he was doing, as if the feel of him after the weeks apart had given her a shock. Then she managed to murmur, "Luke, no...don't do this."

His only answer was to cup her upturned face between his hands and rain kisses over it. She stayed still, not resisting but pleading softly, "For both our sakes...don't."

"I must," he groaned. "It was inevitable the moment I saw you. Don't you know that?"

She gave a little sigh as if admitting defeat. "Yes..." she whispered. "I knew..."

Inside her everything was chaos. She loved him so desperately, but she knew they had no hope. Still her heart pleaded for one last time in his arms, one final loving to live on forever. Her lips fell apart under the demands of his, and he slid his tongue inside her mouth, feeling a surge of delight as he rediscovered its familiar sweetness.

He reached beneath the rough shirt and began to explore her tentatively. Keeping his mouth against hers, he unclasped her bra and drew his fingers along the hollow of her spine, waiting for the tremor that would tell him she still loved to be touched there. To his desperate relief it came, and at the same moment he heard a soft moan escape her.

Emboldened, he slid his hand down beneath the waistband of her jeans. His head spun as he thought of the rest of her, concealed beneath the coarse clothes, waiting for him. He'd been mad to waste time being angry. He bent swiftly to pick her up in his arms and, turning, kicked open the door of the bedroom.

He barely noticed details of the sparse furnishings except for the single bed. He headed purposefully for it and put her down, working urgently on her clothes as soon as his hands were free. He was eager to discover her beloved, remembered body, to see and feel the glow of her skin under his intimate caresses.

She reached up as if to pull his buttons apart, but paused, her face racked with indecision, her eyes searching his face. Luke attacked the buttons himself, casting the expensive garments onto the worn linoleum with as much disregard as he'd once tossed off his shabby working clothes in his eagerness to be naked with her. He was a thousand times more eager now. Eve was his and he had to reassure himself of that.

There was barely room for the two of them on the bed. He pulled her slender, delicate form against his muscular body in a passion of possessiveness, fighting back the desire to take her quickly. He needed all his control now to make this loving the best ever so that she couldn't doubt any longer where she belonged.

He ran his hands over her skin and felt the tremors go through her. Her face had taken on the soft glow that meant his touch had aroused her, and the knowledge inflamed him further, making him pull her tight and crush her mouth urgently with his own. Fires roared through his body, obliterating all anger and injury, obliterating everything except that he wanted this woman. He felt the urgency in his loins and knew that he had to have her.

She was kissing him back, entwining her arms around his neck and burning his lips with her own, feverishly intense, anxious. He dropped his head to her breasts and began to search out one nipple with his mouth, using the tip of his tongue to trace whirls on her skin. The generous fullness of her breasts was like a miracle, given to him anew every time. He'd thought he'd remembered every inch of her, but now he knew his memories had been no more than pale shadows. And perhaps he should be glad of it, because if he'd remembered how beautiful and desirable she really was he'd have gone mad without her.

His mouth had reached the nipple, which stood up, peaked and proud, awaiting him, telling him that she was still eager for his loving. He enclosed it between his lips and heard her moan deeply as he teased it. The knowledge that he had aroused her spurred his own desire to greater heights. He was burning with the need for her, but he forced himself to wait because something vital was still missing. "Do you want me, Eve?" he murmured against her skin.

There was a silence in which his heart almost stopped from fear, but then Eve said, as if the words were wrenched from her against her will, "Yes, Luke, I want you...I want you...take me now..."

"Show me how much you want me," he said in a voice that was half command, half plea.

She understood and took hold of his maleness. He groaned with the wildly pleasurable sensation of her fingers, but greater than pleasure was the relief that she wasn't going to reject him. Shudders racked his body as she guided him to where she was waiting and took him into herself in a movement that was both a surrender and a gift.

He accepted them eagerly, knowing that whatever else happened, nothing in life could be as sweet as union with this woman. He thrust into her slow and hard, trying with every controlled movement to remind her of the shared beauty she'd almost thrown away. At the last moment before their climax came he sought her eyes, wanting to gaze deep into them. But instead of the joy he'd expected they had almost a look of desperation, as though she were asking herself a terrible question. Then she gasped and threw her head back, arching against him again and again, urging him on until his control slipped away and the dark magic possessed them again.

Afterward they lay huddled together on Eve's narrow bed. Luke's arms were wound tightly about her, and his heart was full of gladness. "Thank God!" he said fervently. "We still have each other. It wasn't too late. Get dressed quickly and we'll go home."

When she didn't answer, he turned her face up to his, meaning to kiss her, but something distant and withered in her expression stopped him like a cold hand laid on his heart. "Eve..." he said hoarsely.

He knew what she was going to say even while his frantic mind denied it. She slipped out of his arms and picked up a cotton robe, which she pulled on quickly, as though he must no longer see her nakedness. "I'm not coming back with you, Luke," she said.

"You can't mean that, not after what's just happened. You can't pretend about that. It was real."

"Yes, it was real," she agreed. "I'm not pretending. What would be the use? You know how I am with you. You only have to touch me and I disintegrate inside. When it's over I'm so full of passionate gratitude to you for making me feel that way that I become almost helpless, eager to do anything you want."

"Well, then," he said with the beginning of relief.

"But I mustn't do it this time," she said sadly. "That's why I had to let it happen, to prove to myself that I'm strong enough to love you and desire you, to go up like a bonfire in your arms, and then to send you away. I'm going to need that strength to get through the years without you." Her voice broke on the last word, and she turned quickly away, brushing a hand across her eyes.

He stared at her. What she was saying was too monstrous to be true. While his brain grappled with it he rose mechanically and pulled on his clothes. Eve sank onto the bed and sat with her arms wrapped around herself. She looked huddled and weary, and not at all like a woman who could call the shots with Luke Harmon. But that's what she was doing. Misery and pride warred within him, and pride won. "You used me," he said furiously. "You had no right. You should have stopped me."

"I tried," she whispered.

"Not very hard."

"What would have happened if I'd tried harder? Would you have stopped, Luke?"

He tightened his lips, knowing the answer but ashamed to speak it. After a short silence he said in a harsh, bitter voice,

"You made me think you still loved me and all the time I was part of your private little experiment."

"I do love you," she said huskily. "As for an experiment . . . what about you? You wanted to prove you could make me so crazy with desire for you that I couldn't think straight. But I needed to know that I *can*."

"And having settled that, you're giving me my marching orders," he said furiously. *"Do you think you can do that?"*

"Yes, I can do that, because this is my home, *mine*."

"Until when? How long will it take for high-minded poverty to pall? I know you, Eve. You're used to the best, and pretty soon you're going to want it again. When that day arrives, don't come back to me, because if you do it'll give me great pleasure to throw you out as you're throwing me out."

"I'll remember," she said in a dead voice. "I promise never to come to you for help."

He finished dressing. But in the few minutes it took his rage had given way to a dreary despair. "You said your work gave you happiness," he said. "Can you really be happy without me, Eve?"

She shook her head. "But I can get by," she said simply.

There was nothing more for him to say. He wished he could find some way of helping her financially, but he knew if he offered her money after what had just happened she would never forgive him.

He turned to leave, but at the door she called him back. The sound of her voice saying "Luke," on a pleading note, gave him a pang of hope that made him angry with himself, but he couldn't fight her. He went back to stand in front of her.

She pulled down his head and laid her lips against the scar. "It wasn't that which drove me away," she whispered. "But *that*—" She laid a hand over his heart.

He walked out without looking back.

Mrs. Thompson was hanging about in the front hall, trying without success to look as if she wasn't being nosy. "How much does Miss Chadwick owe you?" he demanded curtly.

"I ain't 'ad last month's rent yet."

"How much?"

She told him.

"It's daylight robbery." Mrs. Thompson opened her mouth to protest but closed it when she saw that he was writing a cheque. "This is two months' rent and I want a receipt."

Eve had left with only a couple of bags. Her extensive wardrobes still contained the clothes Luke had bought her. That night he packed them up. Then he took a scrap of paper and spent an hour trying to write something that would make it impossible for her to return them. At last he settled for: "I send you these because I want no reminders of you in this house."

He added the rent receipt without comment and put the envelope inside the box. The next morning he sent the clothes to her. With luck she would get a good price for them.

Eleven

Luke awoke with a start and found himself sitting up in bed. It was five in the morning, and still dark, but he knew he wouldn't sleep again. This had happened to him often in the two months since he'd seen Eve. There'd been no further contact between them and he'd resigned himself to the dull ache of misery that never left him night or day.

He slept little now, reading papers late into the night, then lying awake for an hour before dropping into a restless sleep that always ended in the early hours. He was haunted by Eve as he'd last seen her, and in his dreams he held her against him as he had during their final lovemaking. Then he awoke to find himself alone, knowing that now he'd always be alone.

He was still in Tyler's room. Once he'd wondered why Tyler, who could afford all the luxury he wanted, had chosen to sleep in this monastic cell with bare linoleum on the floor. Now he no longer wondered. The room's bleakness suited his nature as it must have done for the man who'd sired him.

He'd grown more used to thinking of Tyler as his father since Eve's accusation had forced him to see that their likeness was even greater than he'd thought. But it was a bleak sense of kinship, with no affection in it.

He put on the light and went over to the massive oak dressing table where he kept papers. He took some out of the top drawer and settled down to read. But he couldn't concentrate. Words swam together, and he raised his head, seeking something else to focus his eyes on. His gaze fell on the ugly carving at the back of the dressing table, and he found himself compulsively following its whirls around a set of decorative knobs. After a few minutes he realized that he'd been staring at one of the knobs without seeing it. He rubbed his eyes and looked back.

Now he saw that it was shaped slightly differently than the the others. He began to run his fingers over the carving around it, and to his surprise the wood shifted. He pulled gently on the knob and had a frisson of almost childish excitement as he realized that he'd discovered a secret drawer. He drew it open and found a large brown envelope. Intrigued, he emptied out the contents, and what he discovered made him stare.

There was a small snapshot, the kind that might have been taken with an old-fashioned camera. It showed a young woman sitting on a stone wall. Her unruly hair was blowing about her face, and she was laughing at whoever was behind the camera in a teasing, joyous fashion. Luke had never seen the woman in the flesh, but he'd seen a dozen photographs in Megan's house, and he recognized his mother.

There were two small white envelopes. The flap of one was tucked in, and he opened it to discover a curl of beau-

tiful red hair. That, too, he recognized, for Megan had pre-
served a lock of Helen's hair and shown it to Helen's son.
As a child he'd often held it in his hands, trying to conjure
up the mother he'd never known.

He stared at the picture and the hair, trying to reconcile
his conflicting knowledge. Tyler had had a brief affair with
Helen but turned his back on her when she was carrying his
child. The child himself had been anathema, never to be
acknowledged. But Tyler had kept these mementos until the
end of his days.

Luke looked at the other envelope. It had been sent to
Helen at an address in a nearby town. But that address had
been crossed out and another scribbled in. This, too, was
crossed out. The letter had chased her to five places before
the post office had given up and returned it to the sender.

Suddenly galvanized, Luke tore it open and read the
words Tyler had written to his mother long ago, words she
had never read. As he read he grew very still.

Who could have imagined that bitter old man ever pouring out his heart with such passion? Tyler had written as
though full of terror because he'd seen the meaning of his
life slipping away from him. He'd begged Helen's forgiveness for the mad pride that had made him refuse to marry
her, pleading that he loved her and couldn't live without her.

I know I'm not an easy man, perhaps I'm even a bad
one. I think I must be to have turned away from you
who are everything that is good and beautiful in my
life. It's hard for me to love, or to admit that I love, and
you have invaded my heart so completely that it made
me afraid. But I know that with you there is nothing to
fear. You can defeat the darkness that sometimes
threatens to overwhelm me. But if I lose you forever
there's no hope for me. My darling, what will I be-

come without you? My life is so empty now that you're gone. It took me far too long to understand. Say it isn't too late.

Luke read the letter three times before he put it down and stared into space. Now he knew the history of his father's tortured love for his mother as clearly as if he'd been there to witness it. Through these pathetic, futile words, Tyler had spoken, not to the woman he'd loved, but to the son he'd refused to recognize because the sight of him had hurt too much.

That harsh, inarticulate man had loved Helen more than he could cope with. He'd driven her away, but then realized the dreadful thing he'd done and poured out his heart on paper, the only way he could talk. But it was too late. She'd gone beyond his reach, running from city to city, always one step ahead of the letter that would have brought her back to him.

For Luke had no doubt that his mother would have returned if she'd read Tyler's words, and then, how different everything would have been, not only for himself but also for the lonely man who'd admitted his feelings too late. Instead, the letter had returned unread, and Tyler had hidden it away for the rest of his life while the shell around his heart had grown harder.

He took out the lock of hair again, and as he did so he realized that there was a small sheet of paper with it in the envelope. It bore a few disjointed phrases: "April fifteenth. St. Catherines. London. Too late. *Too late.* The child killed her. He should have died instead."

Luke had been born in St. Catherine's Hospital, London, on April fourteenth. And on that date Helen had died. Now he knew that Tyler had found her, after all, but he'd arrived a day late, when she was beyond hearing any of the things he'd longed to say. And in his anguish he'd turned on his baby son, uttering the terrible wish that the child should have died so that his love might live. And his hatred had never died. Here lay the answer to why Tyler had never softened to him all his life.

Luke dropped his head into his hands, his mind reeling with this new proof of his father's rejection. One question above all tormented him. Megan must have known where her daughter was. Why hadn't she told Tyler?

Then the answer came to him from the depths of his newfound knowledge about himself. The man who couldn't get the words out even to the woman he loved would never have been able to tell Megan. At best he might have barked out a curt demand for information, and Megan, not understanding, would have pretended ignorance to protect her daughter from this seeming bully.

It was speculation but he was sure of it. For he, too, knew the nightmarish sensations of saying all the wrong things. He knew Tyler. He *was* Tyler. And Eve had seen it and fled.

Sanders came straight to the point. "I've got what you want," he said, throwing a file onto Luke's desk. "With what's in there you can send Parry Drummond to jail or just scare the hell out of him, whichever suits you."

"Tell me briefly," Luke said.

"I planted one of my people in his office and she came up with the goods. He's gone in deep with his clients' money again and the market went against him."

Luke glanced at the file, which was full of photocopied documents. His eyebrows rose as he took in some of the contents, and he nodded with satisfaction. "Good work," he said.

"There's one thing more. My agent says he's in a strange mood, very cheerful considering the trouble he's in. She says it's as if he had a private treasure trove. It may not mean anything, but you never know."

Luke left the office and went to his London apartment to study the file in peace. He read long into the evening, and as he read his pleasure grew. The agent had been very thorough and there wasn't a shred of doubt about Parry's guilt. The contents of this file spelt a long jail sentence for his enemy.

He wondered about Parry's mood. Perhaps he thought Eve had other assets that he could call on. If so, the sooner he was put straight the better. He lifted the telephone receiver and dialed Parry's number. "I'm glad you're there," he said when he got a reply. "I want to talk to you. I'll be over in half an hour." He hung up without waiting for an answer.

As soon as Parry opened his front door, Luke knew what Sanders had meant about his strange cheerfulness. Parry was smiling with real pleasure, like a cat that had a nasty surprise waiting for an unwary mouse. "Do come in," he purred. "If you hadn't called me, I was going to call you. You can be useful to me."

Luke surveyed the elegant little mews house with distaste. Its daintiness made him feel awkward. But he'd looked forward to this moment for years and now nothing was going to spoil it for him. "If you think I came here with the idea of being useful to you, you delude yourself," he said coldly.

"I don't think any such thing," Parry assured him languidly. "I'm sure you have some plan to make my life very uncomfortable, and I'm equally sure that you're going to abandon it."

"Uncomfortable is putting it too mildly," Luke said, ignoring the last half of this speech. "You're going to jail, where you belong."

"Dear me, how fierce you sound. I'm all aquiver," Parry said, smiling. "But you know, somehow I don't think I *am* going to jail."

"You'd better start believing it," Luke said. "I have the evidence that's going to put you there. You've been speculating with your clients' money, and this time Eve can't bail you out."

"Ah, yes, darling Evie. How is she these days? I haven't run across her recently."

"No, you haven't taken any interest in her since she sold her diamonds to save your skin, have you?"

Parry shrugged. "I heard she'd left you and changed her way of life. I felt I shouldn't intrude. We shared a beautiful friendship once. I want to keep my memories unsullied. I really couldn't bear to see her in sordid surroundings."

With difficulty Luke restrained himself from going for Parry's throat. "They might be less sordid if you repaid her some of the money you owe," he said dangerously.

Parry giggled, a sound that send a frisson of hate down Luke's spine. "My dear fellow, don't be absurd. Why should I do that? Besides, since you seem *au fait* with my financial affairs, you must know that I can't repay her. In fact, not to put too fine a point on it, I'm on my uppers. I was going to come to you to help me out."

"I see. You think our 'family connection' would make me reluctant to see you in jail. You shouldn't have counted on it."

"But I wasn't counting on it," Parry said plaintively. "Really, you should credit me with a little more sense than that. I've taken other steps to ensure your cooperation."

Luke eyed him narrowly. Something in Parry's impenetrable self-assurance was beginning to get through to him. "What the devil are you talking about?" he demanded.

"I knew I was going to have to do something. It was obvious that you had your knife into me."

"I wonder what could have given you that idea," Luke observed sarcastically.

Parry shrugged. "Since we're alone there's no need to play games about it. You got what you deserved." His face was suddenly full of vicious spite. "It's a pity they didn't finish you off."

"So I wasn't imagining things. It was you I heard laughing."

"Of course it was. I haven't had such a good laugh in all my life. What were you? A laborer who thought he could make his fortune by bedding Evie. You were so sure of yourself that you even dared raise your hand against *me*. Did you think I'd let that go unpunished?"

Luke nodded. "As I thought. Revenge. It had little to do with Eve."

"Eve was mine," Parry said coldly. "Tyler had said so. You had no right even to think of her. Not then and not now. You're still no more than a jumped-up laborer. Whatever you have is built on what Tyler gave you as a payoff."

"At any rate I seem to have handled money rather more astutely than you have," Luke said, refusing to be sidetracked by insults.

"You've had a certain cheap success, and I suppose that's lucky for me. It's time you started paying me back for the trouble you caused in my life. So you've discovered I've been playing with clients' money. So what? I was going to tell you anyway. I need half a million and you'd better come up with it quickly."

"Suppose I prefer the other option, standing back and watching you rot in jail?" Luke enquired.

"Then you'll watch darling Evie rot with me," Parry snapped. "As my partner, she's implicated in whatever I do."

"Since when was Eve your partner?" Luke asked with a dangerous edge to his voice.

"Since a few days after your marriage. She signed some share transfer documents to cover the money from her diamonds. But one of those documents made her a partner in the firm. Luckily she was in too much of a rush to read anything."

"Plus the fact that she trusted you," Luke said softly.

Parry shrugged. "Dear Eve was always too trusting." He laughed nastily. "She's as sharp as they come if it's an Egyptian pot or a piece of ivory, but she can't see through people to save her life. Never could. I've got her thoroughly stitched up. If you send me down, she goes down with me."

For a wild moment Luke wanted to roar with mirthless laughter at his own expense. Here it was, what he'd dreamed of, the chance to destroy both his enemies with one blow. And instead of triumph all he could feel was a terrified churning of the stomach at the thought of Eve in danger.

I should have protected her from this, he thought frantically. *Why didn't I?*

"You little bastard," he said venomously. "She gave her last penny to help you and you turn on her like this."

"Unfortunately it was necessary," Parry said languidly. "I'm going to need money now and in the future and, as you say, she had nothing else to give. That leaves only you. I had to have some method of making you see reason."

Luke made a desperate attempt at bluff. "But you miscalculated. Eve and I have separated. I no longer give a damn what becomes of her."

Parry shrugged and smiled. "In that case you have only to present your evidence to the fraud squad. It'll be interesting to see what she makes of a prison uniform, won't it? I don't think she'll like it somehow. In fact, I don't think she'll like a good many of the things that will happen to her behind bars."

He'd barely got the last word out before Luke's fist connected with his jaw. Parry never saw the blow coming, and it hurled him back against his delicate Chinese silk wallpaper. Before he could recover his breath Luke had hauled him forward for another blow. This one knocked Parry's front teeth in and sent blood streaming down his chin. A third punch sent him crashing into an antique chair that disintegrated under him. Before he could attempt to rise he felt himself hauled to his knees by Luke's hands meeting around his neck.

Luke looked down at Parry's face livid with terror, and a murderous rage filled him, not for his own sake, but for Eve's. "You filthy double-dealing little snake," he grated. "I ought to put an end to you here and now." Parry made a frantic choking noise. "But don't worry, I'm not going to. I need you alive to hand over that paper she signed." Parry emitted another choke, which Luke correctly interpreted. "Oh, yes, you will," he said. "Fetch it, *now*."

He released his hands and Parry collapsed onto the floor, feeling his throat and making a rasping noise. "I'll get you for this," he lisped through his broken teeth. But at the sight of the face Luke turned on him he shrank back screaming, "Keep away from me!"

"Fetch that paper," Luke snapped.

"I haven't got it here," Parry said hoarsely. "It's in my safe at work. It takes two keys to open it and my lawyer has the other."

Luke realized that this was probably true. Parry had anticipated trouble. "Very well," he said, "tomorrow you'll get your lawyer to open it up and you'll hand me that document. If I'm satisfied, I'll make you a once-and-for-all payment that will keep you out of trouble this time.

"But if you or your lawyer try any tricks, I shall take my wife to another country where she'll be safe from British law. Then I'll present my evidence to the police and watch you fry."

"You'll be aiding and abetting a fugitive from the law. It would ruin you," Parry whispered.

"Perhaps. Perhaps not. I think I'd manage to survive. But even if I didn't, I wouldn't care as long as—" Luke stopped himself. He couldn't speak to Parry of the blinding revelation that nothing mattered...not money, not power, not revenge, not life itself...as long as Eve was safe. There was only one person who must hear him say that...and so many other things. "I'll do it," he repeated. "Do I make myself clear?"

Parry nodded and slowly hauled himself to his feet, his gaze fixed on Luke. Suddenly his eyes narrowed, and he reached for a heavy crystal ashtray. Just in time Luke saw it coming for his head and, turning, knocked Parry sideways with the back of his hand. Parry landed in a corner, sprawled like a rag doll, and lay looking up at him with eyes burning with hate.

"That's what I should have done a long time ago," Luke said, and walked out without a backward glance.

Twelve

She'd known. That was the thought that whirled in Luke's brain as he headed his car toward Oakapple Street. She'd known Parry had tricked her somehow.

When had she first suspected? Perhaps on the night when she'd worn the diamonds, when he'd begun to let his mask slip. With Eve in his power Parry had felt safe in taunting both of them, and she'd begun to guess . . . not the details, just that something was wrong with those papers she'd signed. That was why she'd wanted to talk to Brian Parker, why she'd tried to talk to him—she had been trying to find out. But she couldn't ask for his help outright because he wouldn't let her. "Oh, God, don't let me be too late!" he cried out loud.

Every traffic light seemed to be against him until he went half mad with frustration. If only she had a telephone, but he didn't know what he was going to say, except to beg her to forgive him. It would be easier when they were face-to-face.

He'd had no contact with her since their meeting in her little apartment. She'd sent him a note thanking him for the clothes and the help with her rent, but her words had been cool and stilted and he couldn't read an invitation into them.

At last he reached the street, parked hurriedly and ran up the steps. To his dismay he couldn't see any lights on in the attic flat, and when he rang Eve's bell he found that it still made no sound. Frantically he pressed Mrs. Thompson's bell, keeping his finger on it until at last he could hear her coming. "What you doing 'ere?" she demanded suspiciously.

"I've come to see my... Miss Chadwick," he said. "But the bell still doesn't work."

"Wouldn't make no difference if it was. She's gone," Mrs. Thompson announced with grim pleasure.

"Gone where? You mean out for the evening?"

"No, gone. Skedaddled. Kaput. Finished. Paid me a month's rent in lieu of notice and vanished."

A cold hand clutched him, and he had to hold on to the doorjamb. "You mean she's moved out of the flat?"

"Ain't that what I just said? She's gone."

"When?"

"Today." Pleasure at his desperate face made her add cheerfully, "You ain't missed her by much."

"How much?"

"An hour perhaps."

For a wild, hopeful moment he wondered if Eve had gone back to Drummond Lea. "Did she say where she was going?" he demanded tensely.

"She might have. I wasn't taking much notice." Luke produced his wallet and her eyes brightened. "But I dare say if I thought about it..." Her hand closed on the ten-pound note he'd thrust into her palm. "Now I remember. She said she was going abroad. She'd been offered a job."

The bright dream cracked and fell around his feet. Eve hadn't returned to him, after all. "What job, where?"

"Something to do with art?" Mrs. Thompson hazarded hopefully. "And it's abroad, that I do know, because she said she had to dash off to the airport."

"But she must have left a forwarding address," Luke insisted frantically.

With a regretful eye on Luke's wallet Mrs. Thompson admitted that she had no idea where Eve was going to work or live. But she was inspired to add, "Perhaps if you looked around her flat, she might have left a bit of paper behind. Not that I ought to let you, but . . ." She surveyed the notes that had magically appeared in her hand. "I'll get you the key."

The tiny flat seemed very quiet and desolate when Luke entered. With Eve's possessions gone it was even drearier than he remembered, and he felt a pang as he recalled her pride in her shabby little home, her independence. He began to pull open drawers and cupboards, madly seeking some clue, however small. But Eve had cleaned everything out very thoroughly, as if determined to avoid pursuit. A cold sweat stood out on his brow as he realized that she'd vanished without a trace, and he didn't even know in which country to look.

Finally, when he was almost in despair, he picked up a small wicker wastebasket. He'd given it an earlier brief glance, long enough to establish that it was empty. But now a more searching look revealed a tiny scrap of paper caught in the wickerwork. With trembling hands he removed it and uncrumpled it. It was a bank receipt, indicating that on the previous day Eve had changed some English money into French francs.

He raced down the stairs and burst in on Mrs. Thompson. "She's gone to France," he said urgently, "probably Paris if she's working in the art world. Did she say which airport she was flying from?"

"London Airport," Mrs. Thompson announced triumphantly.

Luke ground his teeth. "London Gatwick or London Heathrow? If I'm to catch her, I've got to know which one to go to."

But she couldn't help him. Shivers went through Luke at the thought of what little time he had. Another ten-pound note bought him the use of Mrs. Thompson's phone, and he dialed Passenger Enquiries with hands that shook. Two calls established that both airports had flights to Paris that evening, but the Gatwick one left first by an hour. His frantic pleas to be told if Eve was on the passenger list produced polite but implacable refusals, for reasons of security.

He dashed out to the car. The clock on the dashboard told him that he had just enough time to get to Gatwick. He headed out of London, driving as fast as he dared and praying frantically that he was going to the right place. Once Eve had vanished into Paris it could take him months to track her down, and by then it would be too late. All his instincts told him that if he were ever to win her back it must be *now*, tonight.

Fragments of Tyler's letter came back to him. *My life is so empty now you're gone . . . it took me far too long to understand . . . say it isn't too late . . . too late . . .* Sad words that expressed the emptiness in a man's heart now bore a sinister echo for Tyler's son. He had a moment of fragmented consciousness when the road stretching ahead of him seemed to be his life without her, empty, featureless, leading nowhere . . . like Tyler's.

As he drove voices raged inside his head.

Why did she suddenly decide to go away?

Because she knew Parry would be making his threats soon.

But why didn't she come to me?

Because you told her never to ask you for help.

But she couldn't have thought I'd let her go to prison.

Couldn't she, you fool? Didn't you tell her you'd enjoy throwing her out?

"I mustn't be too late...too late," he told himself out loud.

He broke the speed limit all the way, but even so when he reached the airport he knew he had no time to spare. The announcement board flashed a message: Boarding in Ten Minutes. He hurried to the gate labeled Departures.

"Can I see your ticket, sir?" a man as big as a house asked, barring his way.

"I'm not traveling. I just want to see if my wife has come through here," Luke explained.

"I'm afraid you can't pass without a ticket."

"Just for a few minutes..." Luke's eyes were flickering frantically around him as he spoke, but there was no sign of Eve.

"Sorry, sir. Rules are rules."

Luke wasted no time arguing but ran to the airline desk and pulled out his wallet. "I want a ticket on your 10:30 Paris flight," he said hurriedly.

The woman tapped some keys on her computer. "I'm afraid that flight is full," she said.

At that moment he saw Eve. She was going through the Departures gate, showing her ticket to the man who had barred Luke's way. He dashed away from the desk. *"Eve!"* he called. *"Eve!"*

She was almost out of sight, but at the sound of her name, called out with desperation, she stopped and looked back, frowning, as though she'd heard a voice often dreamt of but never real. But Luke was still hidden by the crowd, and she turned away again.

"Eve!" Luke had reached the barrier, but his way was blocked by two men. "Just let me through for a moment," he pleaded urgently.

"Do you have a ticket, sir?"

"Look, I've no time to... I only want to talk to my wife. Damn you, let me pass!"

Luke's staff would have trembled at that note in his voice, but the two men didn't budge. Their unyielding faces showed that they'd dealt with madmen and troublemakers before. Luke was suddenly frantic. Time was slipping away, taking her with it, perhaps forever. He knew if he didn't get her back this time he'd never get her back, but all his power was useless. Only his love could reach her now.

"Eve," he cried. "Eve, come back!"

After a heart-stopping moment, she halted and looked around, saw him at the barrier and made an instinctive movement toward him, but then stopped. Luke saw her shake her head sadly, as if bidding him goodbye, and turn away again.

"Eve, come back to me. I love you."

She swung back to look at him, astonishment written clearly on her face. She took a few steps nearer, but slowed, torn by indecision.

He began to hurl words out pell-mell. "I've seen Parry, I know what's happened. I can take care of it. Everything will be all right if only you'll come back to me. But if you don't..." He shuddered and lifted his tortured face to her. "Oh, God, if you don't..."

"Luke." Her lips framed the word soundlessly.

"I love you. I can't live without you. Don't leave me. I beg you."

As if he'd touched a spring within her, she began to run back toward him. The men barring Luke's path melted away, giving her a clear path to throw herself into his arms.

Much later that night, when they could spare the time to talk, he said, "Those papers you signed made you Parry's partner. He was going to hold that over our heads."

"I guessed he'd done something like that. That's why I was going away, to leave you free to fight him. It was as though I saw him clearly for the first time. All these years I've thought of him as feckless and immature, but basically decent. Suddenly it was as though a distorting lens had been removed and I realized you'd been right all along. He *was* the one who had you beaten up. I should have believed you."

"That doesn't matter. It's in the past. When I discovered what he'd done, it was as though the world shifted on its axis. Everything I'd thought was important, like revenge against Parry, like pride, was actually trivial. The only important thing was that I loved you, but I'd failed you. And because of that you were in danger." He pulled her tightly against him, overwhelmed with fear at how close he'd come to losing her.

"But aren't I still Parry's partner?" she asked when she could speak.

"Only until tomorrow morning. I'm going to buy that paper from him."

"But suppose he holds it back to blackmail you?"

He gave a grim smile. "Don't worry, he won't. Parry isn't a brave man."

"But suppose he does," she persisted, troubled.

"Then we'll do what I told him—go abroad and fight him from there."

"It would mean starting all over, losing everything you've achieved."

"But I've achieved nothing. I realized that tonight. I was like Tyler, surrounded by wealth but living in a wasteland. I know now that he'd have given up everything in the world if only the woman he loved had come back to him. And I'm my father's son." He held her against his heart. "You're the only thing that matters. Will you promise never to leave me again if I promise never to give you cause?"

But she shook her head. "I promise never to leave you as long as you love me," she said. "That's a much better bargain."

"Yes, because neither of us can lose." He looked down tenderly into her face. "I love you so much, and I've wasted so much time."

"But we have all our lives now to make up for it."

"And even that won't be enough time for everything I want to say, except that words can't say it."

"Then don't try. What do we need with words?"

She kissed him, enfolding him in her profound tenderness, and his heart felt again the peace that only she could give. They'd found each other again, and this time it was forever.

*   *   *   *   *

Silhouette Desire®

1989
IS THE YEAR
OF THE MAN!

What makes a romance? A special man, of course, and Silhouette Desire celebrates that fact with *twelve* of them! From Mr. January to Mr. December, every month has a tribute to the Silhouette Desire hero—our **MAN OF THE MONTH!**

Sexy, macho, charming, irritating . . . irresistible! Nothing can stop these men from sweeping you away. Created by some of your favorite authors, each man is custom-made for pleasure—*reading* pleasure—so don't miss a single one.

Mr. January is Blake Donavan in RELUCTANT FATHER by Diana Palmer
Mr. February is Hank Branson in THE GENTLEMAN INSISTS by Joan Hohl
Mr. March is Carson Tanner in NIGHT OF THE HUNTER by Jennifer Greene
Mr. April is Slater McCall in A DANGEROUS KIND OF MAN by Naomi Horton
Mr. May is Luke Harmon in VENGEANCE IS MINE by Lucy Gordon
Mr. June is Quinn McNamara in IRRESISTIBLE by Annette Broadrick

And that's only the half of it—
so get out there and find your man!

Silhouette Desire's

MAN OF THE MONTH . . .

Silhouette Special Edition

presents

★ LOVE AND GLORY ★

from
Lindsay McKenna

Introducing a gripping new series celebrating our men—and women—in uniform. Meet the Trayherns, a military family as proud and colorful as the American flag, a family fighting the shadow of dishonor, a family determined to triumph—with **LOVE AND GLORY**!

June: A QUESTION OF HONOR (SE #529) leads the fast-paced excitement. When Coast Guard officer Noah Trayhern offers Kit Anderson a safe house, he unwittingly endangers his own guarded emotions.

July: NO SURRENDER (SE #535) Navy pilot Alyssa Trayhern's assignment with arrogant jet jockey Clay Cantrell threatens her career—and her heart—with a crash landing!

August: RETURN OF A HERO (SE #541) Strike up the band to welcome home a man whose top-secret reappearance will make headline news . . . with a delicate, daring woman by his side.

Three courageous siblings—
three consecutive months of

★ LOVE AND GLORY ★

Premiering in **June**, only in
Silhouette Special Edition.

FOUR UNIQUE SERIES
FOR EVERY WOMAN YOU ARE . . .

Silhouette Romance

Love, at its most tender, provocative,
emotional . . . in stories that will make you laugh and
cry while bringing you the magic of falling in love.

6 titles
per month

Silhouette Special Edition

Sophisticated, substantial and packed with
emotion, these powerful novels of life and love will
capture your imagination and steal your heart.

6 titles
per month

Silhouette Desire

Open the door to romance and passion. Humorous,
emotional, compelling—yet always a believable
and sensuous story—Silhouette Desire never
fails to deliver on the promise of love.

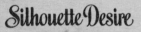

6 titles
per month

Silhouette Intimate Moments

Enter a world of excitement, of romance
heightened by suspense, adventure and the
passions every woman dreams of. Let us
sweep you away.

4 titles
per month

READERS' COMMENTS ON SILHOUETTE DESIRES

"Thank you for Silhouette Desires. They are the best thing that has happened to the bookshelves in a long time."

—V.W.*, Knoxville, TN

"Silhouette Desires—wonderful, fantastic—the best romance around."

—H.T.*, Margate, N.J.

"As a writer as well as a reader of romantic fiction, I found DESIREs most refreshingly realistic—and definitely as magical as the love captured on their pages."

—C.M.*, Silver Lake, N.Y.

"I just wanted to let you know how very much I enjoy your Silhouette Desire books. I read other romances, and I must say your books rate up at the top of the list."

—C.N.*, Anaheim, CA

"Desires are number one. I especially enjoy the endings because they just don't leave you with a kiss or embrace; they finish the story. Thank you for giving me such reading pleasure."

—M.S.*, Sandford, FL

*names available on request

D Silhouette Desire ®

COMING
NEXT MONTH

#499 IRRESISTIBLE—Annette Broadrick
June's *Man-of-the-Month* is Quinn McNamara—a man with a
mission. And beautiful Jennifer Sheridan has jeopardized that
mission. Now only Quinn can get her out alive!

#500 EYE OF THE STORM—Sara Chance
You met Ben Forsythe in *Woman in the Shadows*. Now he's back
in his own story with Cinnamon Cartier—a master at the political
game but a novice at love.

#501 WILDFLOWER—Laura Taylor
Her auto accident was clearly an act of providence, and
handsome widower Grayson Lennox was determined to solve the
mystery of Alexa Rivers, the lovely unwed bride.

#502 THE LOVING SEASON—Cait London
A botched hotel reservation forced Diana Phillips to knock on
Mac MacLean's door. The intimidating rancher seemed more
concerned with his prizewinning chili than her, but not
for long....

#503 MOON SHADOW—Janice Kaiser
Kira Lowell thought she had to protect her half-Indian adopted
son from Joshua Bearclaw. But Joshua didn't want to take just
his boy—he wanted both the woman and the child.

#504 SHARING CALIFORNIA—Jeanne Stephens
Who would have thought a basset hound could bring Annie
Malloy and Sam Bennington back together? But when they
inherited the canine TV star, sharing became a way of life.

AVAILABLE NOW: